William Joseph Madden

Disunion and reunion

William Joseph Madden

Disunion and reunion

ISBN/EAN: 9783741192999

Manufactured in Europe, USA, Canada, Australia, Japa

Cover: Foto ©Andreas Hilbeck / pixelio.de

Manufactured and distributed by brebook publishing software
(www.brebook.com)

William Joseph Madden

Disunion and reunion

DISUNION AND REUNION

DISUNION AND REUNION

BY

W. J. MADDEN

SOMETIME RECTOR R.C. CATHEDRAL, AUCKLAND

" Ut unus omnes unicum,
Ovile nos Pastor regat.'
—Hymn for All Saints

LONDON : BURNS & OATES, Limited

NEW YORK, CINCINNATI, CHICAGO : BENZIGER BROTHERS

1897

PREFACE

In the course of duty, the author gave a series of Sunday evening lectures in the Auckland Cathedral, on a topic largely occupying the public attention for the moment.

The large audiences that came for four-and-twenty consecutive nights to hear those lectures, testified to the eager interest felt in the subject.

There was no intention of publishing these unpretending and somewhat hurriedly prepared instructions. But at their close it was the opinion of many who heard them that for others who did not, and for those not of our faith, it would be useful, and perhaps fruitful, to issue the substance of them in some permanent form.

This task has been attempted in the following pages, in the humble hope that if they cannot conclusively persuade, they will at least lead to further thought and investigation of the great question involved.

The chief aim has been to state plainly, and in a popular way, the *causes* that led to the disruption of Christendom, leaving the reader to judge how very much of the human, and how little of the divine, there was in those secessions from the primal fold.

Other demands, not a few, upon the author's time and attention, left him but little leisure to bestow upon his work that care and finish he would desire, so it must go forth with all its sins upon it.

W. J. M.

AUCKLAND, N.Z.,
Feast of St. Lawrence of Dublin, 1895.

CONTENTS

vii

PART IV

THE CHURCH'S ANSWER TO THE REFORMERS

PART V

THE CHURCH'S FINAL ANSWER TO
THE REFORMERS

DISUNION AND REUNION

PART I

SIGNS AND SYMPTOMS

A TROUBLING spectacle to the religious mind is the well-known prevailing disunion among Christians.

It seems almost unaccountable how it could have come about. It is obvious to every one that Christ our Lord, *to whom all in common refer as the source of their teaching,* could never have given a command to teach things plainly contradictory in themselves.

He could not have commanded one set of men to teach that He is always present in a sacrament under the appearance of a little bread ; and another set of men to teach that He is by no means there, and that to say that He is, is an idolatrous impiety.

He could not have commanded one set of men to teach that Calvary is repeated on the altar ; and another set of men to teach that the Mass, in which the Sacrifice of Calvary is renewed, is a " blasphemous fable."

A

He could not have commanded one set of men to teach that sins are truly forgiven to men by their fellow-men in virtue of His commission and authority; and another set of men to teach that this is a horrible assumption and an unholy imposture.

He could not have commanded one set of men to teach that there are seven sacraments, all necessary for man's spiritual needs; and another to teach that there are only two.

He could not have commanded one set of men to teach that marriage is a sacrament reserved to the control of God and His commissioned representatives; and another set of men to teach that it is but a civil contract in the control of the State.

He could not have commanded one set of men to teach that baptism is absolutely necessary to salvation; and another set of men to teach that it is but a ceremony of initiation and not essential.

He could not have commanded one set of men to teach that a place of purification called Purgatory intervenes between earth and heaven; and another set of men to teach that no such place exists.

He could not have commanded one set of men to teach that a binding and loosing power is possessed by His ministers, whereby an indulgence or a remission of temporal punishments may be granted to those who are still debtors to His justice, though their guilt has been forgiven; and another set of men to teach that this is a human invention and a lie.

He could not have commanded one set of men to teach that no one is excluded from His mercy and the merits of His atonement; and another set of men to teach that, no matter what some may do, they are predestined to eternal reprobation.

He could not have commanded one set of men to teach that His Mother was a Virgin, and should be honoured above all creatures next to Himself; and another set of men to teach that she was not a Virgin, and should not be noticed more than the most ordinary of her sex.

He could not have commanded one set of men to teach that the Bible, as the inspired Word of God, was to be kept under the guardianship of a certain infallible authority which was to be its sole interpreter and sole judge of its component parts and versions; and another set of men to teach that it is in no special custody, and that it is for each man, exercising his private judgment, to interpret it according to his own sense, and to construct therefrom his own religion.

He could not have commanded one set of men to teach that St. Peter was granted a Primacy over the other apostles, and a promise that his faith was never to fail, and that the Church, raised upon him as a foundation, was to stand to the end of time, against every opposing power; and another set of men to teach that there is no Primacy in the Church, and no fixed or unerring guide, and no definite successor to St. Peter.

He could not have commanded one set of men to teach that images of holy things, and relics, and blessed water and candles, and penances and fasts, and abstinence and little formulas of prayer, were all spiritually aidful and conducive to piety; and another set of men to teach that such things are grossly superstitious and derogatory to Christ and His merits.

He could not have commanded one set of men to teach that faith only was not sufficient for salvation, but must be carried into good works and holy living, to be meritorious of eternal life; and another set of men to teach that faith without works justifies.

He could not have commanded one set of men to teach that the private confession of sins to a priest was the means ordained by Him to their forgiveness; and another set of men to teach that this is a most damnable practice imposed by a flagitious priestcraft.

Finally, He could not have commanded one set of men to teach that there is but one only religion represented by the Church He founded, without whose pale salvation is not found — at least for those culpably and consciously outside; and another set of men to teach that one religion is as good as another, and that no one need concern himself about any particular system, since "the Kingdom of God is within" each one's heart and conscience.

Now, it is well and sadly known, that in the hour in which we are, all these contradictory things, and many more, are actually taught in the name and professedly on the authority of Christ. It is also equally well known, on the grounds of the most elementary logic, that one half of these statements must be wrong—unalterably and essentially wrong. And who is doing our Lord the outrage of making Him the author of falsehood? It is a momentous question.

Meanwhile, all these contradictions, made more hideous by the clangorous noise of angry contentions, are most afflicting and perplexing to many a good and pious heart in the Christendom of to-day. But if it be so to them, how puzzling must it be to the on-looking heathen, to whom all the religious bodies in turn send emissaries, inviting them to embrace the saving faith. They naturally ask, "But which?" and thus the way of their conversion is blocked.

Earnest men, in every Christian land, are beginning to feel all this very keenly, and, moved by the
misery of it, they have in various ways and places
been taking steps to see if anything can be done
to stay this disaster—for it is nothing else. They
daily see crowds of men driven by this state of
things into utter listlessness and indifference to
religion, if not into avowed unbelief and atheism.
In the face of this terrible calamity, attempts
have been made with greater or less sincerity and
earnestness to bring together into unity various
religious bodies.

.   .   .   .   .

It will be interesting to trace this movement for
unity in various places in our time. It will be
moreover not uninstructive.

Some twenty years ago an attempt was made,
with considerable earnestness and spirit in Germany,
to bring four systems of Christianity into unity.
The committee formed for the purpose entered into
relations with the Russian hierarchy, the Greek and
Armenian schismatic churches, the Anglicans, and
a body of influential high churchmen, Dutch and
Swiss, who called themselves "old Catholics." Conferences of delegates were held for several successive
years by the banks of the Rhine, at Bonn. Men of
talent and admitted learning from various countries

attended. One great English statesman, relieving the tedium of the " cool shade of opposition," betook himself to this arena of controversy.

As a result, they got as far as admitting all that was done up to and in the eighth General Council of the Church, as a basis for union. They stopped there, because in subsequent councils the Primacy and the infallible authority of the Roman See began to be emphasised and insisted upon. This was too much for their liberality. Those representative men were one and all at the same moment—as the children say, "out" with the Pope. The president was an excommunicated priest. The Anglican delegates were English Church dignitaries with their traditional horror of Rome. The Greek and Russian popes stood on the national question of Constantinople and its œcumenical Patriarch as against the Roman supremacy. The Jansenists of Holland and the Calvinists of Switzerland could not be expected to bow before Baal or Babylon.

Still, for twenty years, though at uneven pace, this strange assemblage held on its way of attempted peace. Its last meeting was held in the old town of Lucerne, in Switzerland. The present Pope was by no means inattentive to these proceedings. There is naturally no one in the world so solicitous for religious reunion as the Pope, and Leo XIII. has many times told the world how near it lies to

his heart. He gave striking proof of it during this
Lucerne conference. Regardless of the slight these
men put upon him by expressly excluding him from
any fruit or share in their scheme, he nevertheless
addressed them an autograph letter full of kindly
feeling and praise for their laudable undertaking,
but at the same time he bade them remember that
their labours would be without result unless they
reckoned with the claims of the Mother Church of
Christendom.

On merely historic grounds the Pope's letter should
at least have commanded their respectful consideration. They, however, received it rudely. They informed the Pope that their stand was taken with the
Church, as they deemed it to be, before the ninth
century. That if he would have part with them
and their inheritance he must repudiate all that
the Church of his predecessors had been doing since
that time; especially must he reject and anathe-
matise the Vatican Council and all its wicked deeds,
and, finally, join with them in their glorious efforts
"to eliminate the corruptions at present prevailing
in the papistic and jesuitical Church of Rome!"
Modesty was evidently not one of the characteristic
virtues of these sages of Bonn. But the Pope was
right. Those twenty years of labour have borne
no result. But any one may see how that haughty
ultimatum to the most considerable Church of all,

necessarily doomed their work for Christian unity to hopeless failure.

.   .   .   .   .

In the year which saw the final closing of the conferences of Bonn, a movement towards reunion was taken up in another and entirely unlooked-for quarter. At this time the greatest industrial Exhibition that, perhaps, has ever been held was under way in the central city of the United States of North America. It occurred to some earnest souls that while the material interests of man were being forwarded on so magnificent a scale, his spiritual interests—the great questions of the soul —its duties and relations to its Creator—should not be neglected. It seemed to them that never before had such a grand occasion offered itself to rally men to the side of religion, and bring them more into union on this vital subject. The prime mover in this great affair, strange to say, was a votary of the stern and rugged Calvinism of the Scotch Presbytery. At the suggestion of this Rev. Mr. Burrows, a comprehensive committee was formed. Its membership was open to all denominations. With great courtesy and liberality —avoiding the mistake of the spiritual magnates of Bonn—the American Catholic Hierarchy were offered representation on this committee. The

Bishops, under the presidency of Cardinal Gibbons, met and deliberated on the matter. They deemed it of sufficient importance to refer it to the Pope. He graciously and willingly accorded his sanction to their acceptance of the invitation, and thereupon two Bishops were told off to represent the Catholic Church on this strangely-mixed deliberative body. The committee was formed and the Bishops attended. Invitations were issued to the heads, not only of the various Christian bodies, but of every known religion in the world, thus widening the scope of the original scheme.

It was singular and significant that these invitations were all but universally accepted. The one exception was the head of the Anglican establishment. He took issue with the wording of the invitation. He was asked to send delegates to a "Parliament of Religions." He refused to admit that there could be such a thing. A parliament of this kind supposed religion to be a debatable subject. Moreover, he protested against the supposition implied in the programme that the Church of Rome was the Catholic Church and the Anglican Church was not. So his Grace of Canterbury would have nothing to say to this assembly, nor would he sanction the attendance of his clergy. However, it went on without him, and went on very well. One hundred and seventy delegates, representing one thousand million two hundred thousand souls, attended from the following widely-distant parts of the earth :—

China sent 4 delegates, representing Taoism, Confucianism, and Buddhism.

Japan, 10, representing Shintoism and Buddhism.

Hindostan, 8, representing Brahminism, Brahmo-Somaj, Jainism, and Parseeism.

Red Indians, Negroes, and Polynesians, 5.

Judaism, 12.

Mahomedanism, 2.

Armenian Schismatics, 2.

Greek and Russian Churches, 4.

Roman Catholics, 18.

Anglicanism and various Protestant Churches, 100, including 18 women.

And at the tail of the hunt came 2 from the Agnostic brethren.

In the words of the invitation, " they were brought together to see if any common platform could be found to unite men in the worship of God and the service of their fellows—to advance the cause of religion in the world and increase its force for good wherever found." The originators of the scheme hoped to achieve an unprecedented feat in harmony. From those assembled elements of hopeless discord they seemed to believe that the great, deep diapason which runs through the natures of all men would rise and swell above the dissonants,

until it forced them into one harmonious chord. A
scarcely hopeful thing. But they attempted the
task with manly vigour, and carried it through with
an enterprise and spirit hardly to be looked for
outside that astonishing country of the States.
For the purpose of this assembly, without a
parallel in history, the great audience hall of the
Exhibition was granted very liberally by the administration. The meetings were so admirably
organised and arranged that there was none of
that confusion or Babel-disorder so freely predicted
by many. Sixteen days were devoted to various
congresses, and practical issue given to separate
deliberations in three public sessions attended by
overwhelming numbers. An eye-witness so un-
sympathetic as the French novelist, Paul Bourget,
who happened just then to be touring for the
Gallic traditional *impressions de voyage*, tells us
that these public sessions were among the most
impressive sights he ever beheld. The 170 delegates occupied the platform. So strange a mingling of costumes was never seen. The scarlet of a
cardinal's robe and the purple of Catholic prelates
were side by side with garments of Oriental Brah-
mins, yellow mantles of Buddhist Bonzes, vestments
of Jewish Rabbi and Shinto idol keepers, while
the sombre broadcloth of the separated Christian
ministry discreetly subdued the tone of the brighter

and varied hues. The vast hall was filled to its capacity of 5000 spectators. Here no debate was permitted. There was no voting. There was a calm dignity—an attitude of mutual respect. Each delegate or head of a religion read or spoke his statement without interruption, and often with applause. The utmost urbanity and forbearance marked the proceedings. To Cardinal Gibbons was assigned the office of reciting the opening prayer. The appointment was unquestioned. He stood forward and simply repeated the " Our Father " for that great concourse. It was received with universal approval, and greeted with a cordial Amen. Two hymns were then rendered, one—Cardinal Newman's " Lead, kindly Light," the other—Adams' " Nearer to Thee, O God," and with the same respect and approval.

As the proceedings went forward, it was perceived with satisfaction that the sentiments of all were at one on certain great points—the Fatherhood of God and the brotherhood of men, on benevolent and beneficent charity to all, on the desire for moral good and the need of combating moral evil ; on the necessity of prayer and the utility of sacred melody.

All sections of the assembly seemed to acquiesce in these, but by the Christian portion it was heard with pleased surprise that the Orientals gave testimony to the acknowledgment of Monotheism in their various countries. A priest from Nikho, the chief shrine of Japan, declared for the supremacy of the one eternal God, and explained that the kami, or demi-gods, were held only in the light of agents, subordinate to Him, coinciding, in fact, with the Christian belief in angels.

It was attested that for sixty years in Hindostan all the enlightened teachers have been advocating purer and simpler notions of the Deity, and endeavouring also to wean the people from their absurd idea of the three and thirty millions of divinities and from the cruel and impure rites of their worship. These present-day reformers are called the Brahmo-Somaj, that is, the Society of God. A delegate of this society one day rose up in this Chicago Parliament of Religions, to astonish and delight the great audience. His name was Chundar Mahoumdar. He was a man of about fifty years of age, with a solemn dignity of carriage and a striking personal presence of purely Oriental type. He soon revealed qualities of mind and soul more striking still. His eloquence proved of the very highest order. His sentiments soared to a high plane of spirituality. A few sentences from his remarkable address will illustrate this :—

" Self-restraint, or renouncement of self, is but a part of the spiritual training of the will. The other part is submission—consecration of self to the will of God and the service of humanity. Self-discipline is but a means to a higher end — to submit ourselves and identify ourselves to the will of God. The grain of wheat falls into the ground and dies there before it yields the hundredfold; even so man must give his life for God to keep it for eternity. Death, which is only the destruction of the carnal self, has been, and ever shall be, the price of attaining to God. Who is it was able to say, 'Not My will, but Thine be done'? He only who wrestled with agony to the last bitter drop in the cup—He only who thought of serving God and man when His murderers were waiting at the door. Call that renouncement—call it stoicism—call it death, the fact remains that he only who dies to self can find rest in God and reconciliation with man. This great law of self-denial, of suffering and death, has for its symbol that mystic cross which is so dear to you and dear also to me. Christians! will you for ever repudiate your Calvary? The union of will and character with God is the highest of unions because the most difficult."

Strange and eloquent words indeed from the heart of India.

A Jewish rabbi also was heard to pass a high eulogium on our Lord, a noteworthy sign of soft-ened prejudice on the part of a descendant of the

scribes and doctors. And it was another Jewish
rabbi who recited as the closing prayer the self-
same "Our Father," with which the Cardinal of
Baltimore opened the Congress. He must have
known who composed that beautiful prayer.

The great politeness and peace which marked
the whole course of these proceedings, and the
friendly interchange of ideas among men of widely
differing creeds, delighted every one, and prepared
the way for the scene of wild enthusiasm at the
close. Part of the concluding ceremony was the
rendering of the " Alleluia " from Handel's
" Messiah," by a large and specially trained choir.
When they ended with the refrain—

> "Alleluia, the Lord reigneth for ever,
> For ever shall He reign the King of kings
> And the Lord of lords. Alleluia "—

the immense audience rose as one and cheered
again and again. The women waved their hand-
kerchiefs and wept for joy. The delegates then,
in sight of all, bade each other a parting word, and
the great Congress of Religions was over.

To say that the Parliament of Religions had
achieved with complete success the purpose for
which it had assembled would be to say what could
not be true. Nevertheless it is true to say that in
many ways it was successful. The labours of the

special committee on religious books will no doubt effect much private and quiet good. The Committee agreed upon a list of fifty of the best books on religion, which the management decided to have republished in a cheap, popular form, and circulated in every part of the world. If, on their distant ways, these but bring peace and light to a few troubled hearts here and there, this singular and novel venture to solve the most puzzling of problems will not have been made in vain.

Whatever may or may not be its practical outcome, there is one thing at all events that gives occasion for rejoicing. The Parliament powerfully testified to its universal desire that the entire human family should be more united in the great duty of religious worship. It was felt too that men of opposite beliefs had been drawn closer to each other in the ties of charity, that the barriers and outworks of antagonism and repelling hatred had been carried and in part broken away, that the great longing for union in religious brotherhood, so long felt and silent, had at length found voice, and on the whole a great moral effect had been produced.

On the return of the Japanese delegates, the Mikado was so impressed with what they had to tell him, that he ordered a similar congress to assemble for the purpose of securing religious uniformity for Japan, and of deliberating upon the

best religion to be adopted with a view to that end.
The recent war with China hindered his design;
but it was a tribute to the wisdom and temper of
the Chicago Parliament.

.   .   .   .   .

The action of the present Pope in promoting the
recent Eucharistic Congress at Jerusalem may also
be reckoned as an effort for unity. He hoped by
this means to reach the Eastern schismatic Churches,
and employed the common belief in the Real Presence as a basis upon which to treat for their
return. He confided this important affair to the
prudent and able hands of a distinguished member
of the Sacred College, the venerable and scholarly
Mgr. Langenieux, Archbishop of Rheims. For the
purpose of this congress, as many as 3000 pilgrims
assembled at Jerusalem from every Christian pro-
vince of the Levant, under his presidency. The
offer tendered on behalf of the Pope to the separated
Easterns was, that ritualistic usages, sanctioned by
ancient custom, and disciplinary practices in use,
should be respected and authorised. But when it
came to exacting the acknowledgment of the Primacy of the Roman See as a return for such liberal
concessions, the old Eastern prejudice revived and
divided their counsels. The outcome of this long
conference was the return of some few of the Bishops
to the unity of the Roman Church, but the terms

proposed did not find general acceptance. Still, a preparation of the way has been made, which, no doubt, will bear further result in the near future, especially as this manner of congress has been repeated in Europe, and is to be renewed from time to time.

It is worthy of note too that just about the time of the first Eucharistic Congress, the long negotiations between the Vatican and the Court of St. Petersburg, relative to diplomatic representation, were happily brought to a close by the appointment of a Russian ambassador accredited to the Papal Court—a *rapprochement* little expected from the Russians.

.   .   .   .   .   .

Besides what we have above recorded, it is worth while now to note certain signs which have been appearing here and there during the last decade or more of our times, indicating a kindlier spirit prevailing among the religiously separated in Europe.

Family quarrels are said to be the longest and bitterest. They are also the most blamable. But time softens feelings, the need of mutual aid before a common danger draws the sundered together, recriminations cease, bitterness is forgotten, and thus half the battle for reconciliation is won. Religious dissensions may in some sense be com-

pared with family quarrels, and ought to run the
same course under the same curative law of time.
We have evidently got to the *forgetting* stage and
the season of softened feelings, as the following
incidents may show.

Remembering the long fierce struggle between
Prince Bismarck and the Catholic Church, and the
longer icy silence and haughty coldness of the
Prussian dynasty to all things Papal, the *volte-face*
of the Imperial Chancellor at the time of the Caro-
line Islands discussion was viewed by the world with
a kind of puzzled wonder. Nothing could have
been more frank or cordial than the request made
to the Pope to arbitrate between Spain and the
German Empire, and nothing more gracious than
the Pope's acceptance. The Prince and his Imperial master not only abided loyally by a decision
unfavourable to their contention, but gave expres-
sion to a kindly gratitude to the august arbitrator
by the offer of decorations conferred only on those
of royal rank or of the most distinguished merit.
While among the multitudinous orders heaped upon
the great Chancellor, and perhaps amongst not the
least prized, may now be found one of the highest
in the usage of the Pope to bestow.

The Emperor Frederick of the short reign—many
think too short reign—is accredited with a nobility
of character much beyond the common. He cer-

tainly showed some of it in his always kind relations and considerate sympathy with the occupant
of the Vatican.   The world knew nothing of this
until it came out in the fatal hours when the great
soldier-prince lay sick unto certain death in the
Riviera.   The messages then between the Vatican
and the Prince's household had the frequency and
warmth of old friendship, while the gratitude of his
gifted consort, the Queen's eldest daughter, for the
Pope's solicitude, found frequent and almost filial
expressions in her personal letters.

It may be that this kindly feeling of the mother
counts for much in the strange and almost eager
courtesy with which her son, the present Emperor,
has treated the Holy Father.   His little human
respect before the Italian Government—before all
Europe, for that matter—in paying official visits to
the Pope on two different occasions, departing for
the purpose from the Quirinal and setting out from
the home of his ambassador, as if from German
territory, did infinite credit to his courage, and
bespeaks a greatness of heart and mind not yet
properly appreciated.   Nor has his reverent and
friendly feeling stopped there.   In a public autograph letter he has thanked and complimented the
Pope on his Encyclical Letter about the labour
question, while out of deference to him he has
caused the remaining harassing restrictions on the

German Catholic clergy to be completely removed.
And yet again, the present Imperial Chancellor,
personally appointed by him, is a Catholic. These
are surely signs of the times!

The great strategist, Von Moltke, was known as
the silent man with few friends. It is now known
that one of those few, and the most intimate, was
a Catholic Bishop. Moreover, Von Moltke has left
on record his opinion that the Reformation was a
blunder and an excess.

If we turn to England we there find signs no
less striking, of a more tolerant and kindlier feeling towards the Mother Church. When we reflect
that little more than a hundred years ago it was
death for a Catholic priest to be found on British
soil, and while the angry agitation against a
Catholic hierarchy, which culminated in the foolish
"Ecclesiastical Titles Bill," is as but a memory
of yesterday, some facts of recent occurrence are
indeed expressive of a surprising change. People
of good memories had need to shut their eyes when
reading that Cardinal Manning, in his scarlet robes,
adorned a garden-party of the Prince of Wales, an
event which happened not once, but many times.
And remembering what they knew they may have
leant their hearing for an angry popular outcry at
this; but none was heard. This is all the more
remarkable, since it was well known that this

Cardinal was once an Anglican Church dignitary, and had abandoned, or, as they would say, apostatised from the national religion.

For a dozen years and more before his death, his Eminence was very much in evidence in English public life, and far from being shunned or reviled, he was welcomed and applauded. He was welcomed on the platform among all sorts and conditions of representative men in advocacy of the Jewish cause, and delighted every one, as he outshone them all, by his sympathetic eloquence on that occasion. He gained the nation's praise, and carried off the prize of fame from all his Anglican Church friends by his skilful settlement of the disastrous dockers' dispute.

Some twenty years ago a kind of learned symposium used to be held in London, under the name of the Metaphysical Society. It was composed of men of all colour and no colour in religion—all of them distinguished in their various walks of life. The Cardinal was a leading figure at their social board. Though he made it a point to be always late for dinner, he was in time for the feast of reason, and more than once was chairman of the post-prandial discussions. It was strange, too, and significant, to see in their gatherings a sprinkling of Jesuits from Farm Street, and Fathers of the Oratory from Brompton, freely

mingling with men of such diverse opinions as John
Ruskin, Frederic Harrison, Professor Huxley, Dr.
Martineau, Tyndall, the Duke of Argyll, Mr. Glad-
stone, Lord Tennyson, Dr. Ward, and others not
less known to literature and science. Only a
very great change of feeling made such meetings
possible.

During one of her Majesty's winter sojourns
in the south of France, it was duly recorded in
the press of the country that she paid a visit to
the famous monastery of the *Grande Chartreuse*.
She not only accepted the hospitality of the good
monks, but had, moreover, to receive a special
dispensation from the Pope to permit her to do
so, as by virtue of the monastic rule, no woman
can enter the cloistered precincts. There was a
time within living memory, when such a proceeding on the part of Royalty would have evoked
angry protest from all Protestant England ; yet it
passed without one unkindly comment.

The present writer has it from one of the Jesuit
Fathers on the staff of their college at Beaumont,
near Windsor, that he has seen the Queen, more
than once, drive up the avenue of an afternoon and
walk into their parlour to have a friendly chat
with the Father Superior. Not long since such
a thing would have cost her her crown and her
head. Nowadays nobody passes remarks on it.

Among the crowd of envoys from foreign courts that thronged the Hall of State at Buckingham Palace, bearing congratulatory greetings to her Majesty on the occasion of her golden jubilee, the stately figure of an Italian prelate, Archbishop Ruffo Scilla, attended by a brilliant suite, was not the least noticeable or the least warmly received as he laid the Pope's kindly message before the Queen. And yet even Exeter Hall was silent!

A grand-daughter of the Queen was recently married to one of the Catholic Hohenzollern Princes. For this marriage the Pope granted a dispensation, and it was celebrated at High Mass in the ancient stronghold of Sigmaringen, by the Catholic Bishop of the place. It will be remembered that the leading illustrated journals of London placed pictures of this important event before the eyes of Protestant England, in which the Heir Apparent, numerous members of the Royal Family and of the English nobility on one side, and on the other the German Emperor and his suite, were seen present at Mass—that " blasphemous fable " of the Thirty-Nine Articles. Yet no monster indignation meeting was held as in the bad old days.

The tone of the English Press towards most things Catholic has been correspondingly modified. There was not a dissonant note in the chorus of praiseful obituaries when Cardinal Manning

died. It paid flattering compliments to his successor on his appointment, and took it as honour
done to the nation when he, too, a member of an
old and well-known English family, was raised to
the dignity of the sacred purple.

For the first time since King Henry broke with
the Pope, we have witnessed the despatch of a
special envoy, Mr. Baden Powell, to the Papal
See, to treat about the Church affairs of Malta.

It has been ascertained by those who attend
to English Catholic statistics, that within the last
fifty years twelve hundred Church of England
clergymen have become Catholics, and most of
them priests.

If we look across the Atlantic, to the greatest
and largest branch of the English-speaking family,
similar evidence of more friendly and tolerant
feeling among the religiously separated may be
found.

There are few men in all that great country
of America held in such universal esteem as
the present Cardinal of Baltimore. Without a
solitary protest, he was accorded the most pro-
minent place in that wonderful assemblage—the
Parliament of Religions.

More than once the gifted and versatile Bishop-
President of the New Catholic University has
had the honour of being invited to address the

alumni of Harvard. A Catholic, robed as a Roman prelate, orating in this erstwhile seat and centre of New England Puritanism, is truly an eloquent testimony to the changed and tolerant spirit. The Archbishop of St. Paul's, in the West, through his eloquent advocacy of the temperance cause, has gained the ear and sincere goodwill of all the dissenting religious bodies throughout the country—a thing most difficult to accomplish, for they were the most prejudiced of all against the Catholic Church.

There is not a Catholic educational establishment throughout the United States but has children of Protestant parents, of all denominations, among its boarders. Protestants no longer fear to commit their offspring, in the most impressionable period of their lives, to the care of priests and nuns.

The conversions to the Church from the ranks of the Protestant clergy, as well as from the laity, equal, if they do not exceed, those in England.

It is impossible not to recognise the significance of facts like these. If they are not the prelude to a speedy reconciliation among parted Christian brethren, they are certainly indications of a gradual process, which in time to come will bring it about as nearly as human vicissitudes may permit us to expect.

PART II

THE CAUSES OF CHRISTIAN DISUNION

I.—The Greek Schism

In seeking the causes of religious disunion, we must now change the scene from our own place and time to the city of Constantinople, in the middle of the ninth century.

The natural beauties of that famous capital were the same then as now. The same Golden Horn curved out into the Bosphorus, whose waters laved the wooded slopes where stood the Imperial Palaces, now called Seraglio Point. The city rose from the busy harbour—the mart of the world—and spread over the undulating hills. Its fine edifices and sumptuous homes were well suited to the wealthy and prosperous capital of a still great Empire. But the numerous churches, the monastic and conventual buildings crowning its hills—above all, the gilded dome of the splendid basilica of St. Sophia, with the cross raised above it, proclaimed it a great Christian city, too. There were no Turks there then. A Catholic and Christian city it had been for 500 years since the Emperor Constantine, after whom it is called, transferred the seat of Empire from Rome. Its unrivalled climate and beauty of situation, besides its central and commanding position between the East and West, were supposed to have largely influenced him in changing the capital. But he is credited too, and rightly, with a higher motive in taking the Imperial throne so far away from Rome. He wished to leave that city to the Popes. The Popes he was now to revere, and did revere, as his spiritual superiors, and he could not but have felt that they would be freer to govern the universal Church when not under the shadow and the influence of an imperial court. Non-Catholic historians have scoffed at this statement, and flouted it as a fable. But what more natural for a recent and fervent convert than to do this, especially one with the genius and foresight of Constantine the Great. And the pious-minded have never feared to say that it was a step guided by the directing hand of Providence. It was the wisest provision that could be made for the head of the Church. For most of the troubles that have beset the Church in various times and places have come from too close proximity to courts and rulers, as this very case of the Greek Church, in the times of which we are about to treat, only too clearly proves. This is why the Popes have always contended for personal independence

through all time.   Though every inch of territory
has been taken from him in our day by force of
arms, and men have sought to count him but as a
unit in a kingdom, he has never admitted, and never
will admit, that he is the subject of any ruler.   The
affairs he administers by divine commission concern
the people of every country, hence it is most necessary that he be free from the controlling influence
of any one.   God has ruled it so hitherto, and we
believe He will so rule it to the end whatever men
may succeed in doing for a time to frustrate His
plans.

Constantinople and all the Eastern Provinces it
ruled had been in strictest union with the See of
St. Peter, at the time of which we now speak, for
500 years.   It had been the scene of more than
one General Council of the Church, held by command of the Pope, and presided over by his legates.
Its Patriarchs held their appointment from the Pope,
and always acknowledged his primacy of jurisdiction,
and as yet there was no break in Christian unity.
But now came a disturbance of that peace which all
these long centuries have not restored.   It came
from a cause so local and trifling, so outside any
doctrinal dispute, that we probably never would
have found it detailed as history, were there not at
hand one of those restless and ambitious men of
genius who seized it to forward his own designs.

This is one of those cases which illustrate that patient and mysterious divine permission by which the free action of men can intervene to mar the dearest interests of God in this world until the fulness of His time comes for the reckoning. With the free play of the human will He rarely interferes in any visibly miraculous manner, no matter how greatly it may be abused, or what mischief and wreck it may bring. But it is a dangerous faculty. And if men would but remember that He will be there at the end of things to demand an account, they would never permit themselves to be lulled into false security by a temporary success of their will against the will of the Omnipotent, and human souls would be saved from many a misery.

The actors in this Eastern drama were all exalted personages. They were : The widowed Empress Theodora, a lady of culture, of prudence, and true piety ; her boy, the future Emperor, a lad of dull mind and feeble will ; Bardas, his uncle, and brother of the Empress, a man of corrupt morals and un-principled character ; Ignatius, the saintly Patriarch of the Imperial City ; and Photius, an accomplished courtier of commanding ability, only equalled by his boundless ambition—to appear later on the scene.

The action of the drama opens on the Feast of the Epiphany. The congregation is pouring through the open doors of the cathedral on the

conclusion of High Mass. It breaks into groups
as they go along discussing with bated breath the
extreme measure taken by the Patriarch just now
in the Church : he had publicly refused to give
the Holy Communion to Bardas—Bardas, the most
powerful man in the Empire. Trouble was sure to
come of this. They knew a good many bad things
of Bardas, but what had he done now ? and so forth.
They were instructed enough, however, to know
that such action as the public refusal of the sacraments was only taken with notorious scandal-givers
who, though admonished, neglected to amend, and
that such Bardas must have been. Few there were
who did not commend and admire the Patriarch's
high and courageous sense of duty in not making
any distinction of persons where distinction was
unlawful. Troubled and in tears, the Empress re-
pairs to the palace. Her son Michael treats the
matter as food for laughter ; but she checks his
levity, reminding him how she often warned him
not to be misled by his unscrupulous uncle, whose
reckless conduct was a constant source of pain to
her and a scandal to her people ; that he was
clearly bent on ruining him—Michael—by encour-
aging him in idle pursuits and every indulgence ;
that the Patriarch had no option but to act as
he had done, and therein had her entire approval. The stupid boy little relished the lectures

of his pious mother, so he betook himself to his
uncle to discover what he had to say on the situation. He found him pacing his apartment, chafing
and raging like a caged animal. The news this
jibing boy bore him from his mother did not tend
to calm the storm. Bardas, who was a general and
chief in command of the troops, had full power to
give effect to his wrath. When he heard of the
Empress's adverse opinion, he decided on the boldest
measures. He had her instantly seized and conveyed with her daughter to a neighbouring convent,
and immured under guard. He at the same time
published that her Majesty had freely abdicated
in favour of her son, and had entered religion, in
accordance with a desire she had long cherished to
that effect. The Patriarch Ignatius, however, knew
better than this. Well aware of the sore cost to
himself, he stood in defence of these wronged and
defenceless women. He exposed the falsehood of
this story, and would have rallied the people on the
side of the Empress had not the watchful Bardas
been beforehand with him. Just as promptly as
he executed the seizure of the Empress, he hurried
the venerable Archbishop from his palace and imprisoned him on an island in the Bosphorus.
Strange time and strange condition of society when
such high-handed crime could go unchecked without
a struggle. But an army, and a treasury out of

c

which to pay it, account for most of the crooked
things of history.   And Bardas had both.   Besides,
there was no Press then, and no public opinion, and
what was done in high places concerned little the
run of men, provided their small private interests
were untouched.   Moreover, by proclaiming the
pliant Michael Emperor things were made to wear
a legal look, and the age had not yet dawned when
popular movements could avail against despotic rule.
Not daring to kill the Patriarch, Bardas now used
every means to coerce him, but in vain.   Cruelty
was tried.   Kindness was tried.   Liberal offers of
pension and honoured retirement were made, all to
no avail.   He stood firm, not so much for his own
rights, for he was a man of saintly character, but
for the rights of the Church that had been outraged
in his person.

The violent conduct of this tyrant Bardas by
the overweight of its injustice might in time have
defeated itself and a remedy been found, had there
not been one behind the scenes ready and able to
aggravate and prolong this crying and cruel situation.   *This man was Photius.*   There was no one
of his time, and but few among all the children of
men, so richly gifted as he.   High birth and ample
means were his.   A fine presence and courtly bearing added irresistible charm to a cultivated affability
of manner, which made him universally popular.

His mental endowments excelled even his external advantages. These he assiduously disciplined by close application. There was no branch of such learning as prevailed in his time that he had not mastered. But oratory, that greatest and rarest of human powers—that indispensable hand-maid of ambition, and also most powerful engine for good—was his special and favourite pursuit. With him, as with others, the pride of high and keen intelligence, and delight in exercising a facile and superior mind, blunted the grosser taste for coarser pleasures. He never dissipated. His young as well as his mature years were serious. To perfect his eloquence, he became a teacher of it. His school, which was frequented by the youth of the Imperial City, provided him with opportunities for oratorical displays. He became the most eloquent, as well as the most learned man in Byzantium or out of it. He was also the most agreeable and accomplished. He was a linguist and a musician. But nothing human is perfect. Even he had his flaw. It was that peril and rock to all the gifted —the evil spectre that strides by the path of glory, veiling the eyes and beclouding the minds of the greatest men, urging them into the quagmires of mis-takes, failure, ruin. He had overweening ambition.

But what brought this man of genius, with so bright a worldly career opening before him, to have

aught to do with Church affairs. Church affairs
are generally far from the dreams and schemes of
such as he. Men like Photius usually fly at higher
game. They usually contemn a lot so tame and
lowly in their eyes as a cure of souls. The unen-
ticing path of spiritual things repels them. The
prize of the Imperial Purple, or at least, a place
of power near the throne, ought rather to have
appealed to the intriguing resources of a Photius.
He himself, probably, would have been the last
to think of Church preferment. He was a layman,
already in his prime, and hitherto no sign of the
call divine had been at all exhibited in his character
or his conduct; yet when the offer of the Patriarchal
Chair in the room of Ignatius was made him, he
did not greatly hesitate to accept. He took it to
oblige a friend. Bardas was the friend. Bardas
was more; he was his admirer, his flattering patron,
and his intimate companion. In his secret heart,
maybe, he held him in the light of a formidable
rival for power in the State, and here was a good
chance to remove him for good and all from the
political arena. For another thing, with Photius
for archbishop, he should have no fear of reprimand
and public censure. Photius would never be so
inconveniently pious as to refuse him the sacrament
when it suited his purpose to approach.

On his side, Photius found not a little to tempt

him in the offer. The Patriarchate was a place of great power and distinction, second only, in those days of faith, to the Imperial throne, and in honour and reverence before the people not second even to that. The patronage was extensive, the revenues very large, and more than a hundred Bishops were suffragan to its jurisdiction.

Thus was this high and sacred office made the sport and plaything of these designing men. Had there been the least nobility of character about this Photius, he would have scorned to intrude into the place of which a saintly and persecuted old man had been so unjustly and so cruelly deprived. Had any high sense of honour been his, he would have shrunk from any part in the schemes of men so vile and lost as Bardas and his nephew. But ambition stays not to parley with either nobleness or honour.

No sooner did he give his consent than, with indecent and unprecedented haste, this layman was hurried, in the space of a few days, through all the grades of sacred orders, and, without any reference to the Supreme Pontiff, proclaimed Archbishop and Patriarch of Constantinople.

This could only have been effected by the co-operation of an unworthy and suspended Bishop whose case was actually under consideration in Rome just then. This was a certain Gregory, who had

formerly been consecrated for the see of Syracuse.
This see, though so far removed, was within the
jurisdiction of Ignatius as Metropolitan. When
the nomination came before him, he refused to
ratify it, as he had evidence that this man was
unfit, and had used underhand and unworthy means
to secure his election. His case was referred to
Rome, where he was declared provisionally suspended until all doubt should have been cleared up.
He had come to Constantinople to make interest
for his cause at the court. He soon became the
friend of Bardas and Photius, and gradually gained
many adherents among the clergy, and even among
the Bishops, who, thinking the rule of Ignatius
too rigorous, had grown unfriendly to him and indifferent to his sufferings. He it was who, with
these clerical followers, took part in the ordination
and consecration of Photius.

It is to be deplored that no protest of any
weight came from the great body of the clergy or
the numerous Bishops of this Eastern Church
against these unwarrantable and manifestly illegal
proceedings; and it must be admitted, however
regretfully, that they must have been in a very
supine and nerveless condition—too near and too
dependent on the powers of State.

The few who did stand for right and justice to the
deposed Patriarch only drew upon themselves his fate

—deposition and deportation. There was but one power which could have coped with this great wrong in the beginning, and that was the authority of the Roman Pontiff, which as yet, at all events, was acknowledged and obeyed through the whole extent of the Church. Photius was far too well informed a man not to have known this, and too clear not to have thought out his plan for reckoning with it and anticipating its action. He resolved to open the question himself. He induced the Emperor to send two envoys to Rome to inform the Pope of his appointment, and pray for its confirmation. He made them the bearers of a special message and greeting from himself to the Holy Father. He spoke in a minor key of self-depreciation. He declared that on the *voluntary resignation* of his worthy predecessor, the high honour had been thrust upon him, though most unwilling and fearful of his own unworthiness and the great responsibility, and piously commended himself to the clemency and prayers of the Father of the Church—all this in a flowing and gracious style, such as no other man knew better how to pen. He saw to it that this embassy should be both brilliant and imposing. He spared no expense. Provided with a numerous attendance, and laden with rich presents for the Papal Court, they set out Romeward.

Meanwhile, the lawful Patriarch was in exile,

his mouth closed in prison, where, it is said, he
was kept in chains. The usurper, always a lover
of lavish display, now made it his task by a show
of magnificence to gain the popular favour. · He
kept up a regal state. He was splendid in his
entertainments, at which the Emperor and Bardas
were frequent guests. He scattered gifts and
money with an open hand, until his admirers and
parasites were legion. At the same time he af-
affected, externally, a great zeal for religion. He
added great splendour to all Church ceremonial.
He despatched missionaries to win to Christianity
the wild hordes of the Bulgari and the Sclaves, who
had descended from the north and threatened the
borders of the Empire in arms. Before the people
he was the popular, the brilliant, the zealous prelate,
and his friends hoped that the austere and ascetic
Ignatius would quickly pass from the popular
remembrance.

In those days it was a far cry from Constantinople to Rome, so that the usurper had ample
time to thus establish his position before the Pope
could learn anything of what had transpired, or take
evidence as to the true state of affairs. At the
same time it is important to note that the embassy
despatched by Photius to Rome with his version
of the matter, is a historical fact of great value.
It is an undeniable testimony from the Greeks to

the supremacy and primacy of the Holy See, which
nobody, up to this, had thought of questioning.

The advent of so distinguished an embassy caused,
as may well be imagined, no inconsiderable stir in
Rome. Had the occupant of the Papal See been
a man easily dazzled by Imperial favour, or caught
by flattering gifts and smooth words, he would
eagerly have met so condescending an advance,
and readily conceded the Imperial demands in this
matter of Church government. But such was not
the man who then filled the chair of Peter.
Nicholas I. was a great Pope, full of wary prudence, knowing no interest but God's reign in souls,
and steadfast in the cause of justice and right.
He received the envoys with every mark of respect
due to the emissaries of the head of the Empire.
He treated them with royal hospitality. He read
their despatches and listened to their pleadings.
But something prompted him to wait. Perhaps,
like the Trojan hero, he feared those "gift-bearing
Greeks." Besides, if Ignatius had really resigned,
as represented, he would be sure to apprise him
of his grounds for so important a step. Though
he had no reason to question the plain and full
statement contained in the Imperial messages, yet
he was not easy about the matter. The situation
was a difficult and delicate one. It would be
ungracious and even dangerous to send a refusal

back by the envoys; it would look like doubting
the Imperial word to ask for evidence in corroboration, while it would be great imprudence to say
yes to everything. Only a firm man could solve
the difficulty as Nicholas did. He composed two
letters, one for the Emperor and the other for
Photius. They were gracious and paternal. He
gave them full credit for the respect they had
shown him, and the zeal for religion with which
they accredited themselves. At the same time he
firmly informed them that the sense of his high
duty did not permit him to decide on the business
submitted off-hand, that it was the usage of the
Supreme Pontiffs before deciding important matters
in distant parts of the Church to send special
legates first into the place to report thereon. He
felt it necessary to do so on the present occasion,
and, therefore, had appointed two Bishops to proceed on this mission to Constantinople, and he
gave their names, Rodoald and Zachary, Bishops of
the sees of Portua and Anagni. These letters he
entrusted to the envoys, whom he dismissed with
the marks of honour and goodwill with which he
had received them.

This arrangement did not at all suit Photius
and his Imperial patrons. But, seeing that it
was inevitable, as the legates would be already
on their way, they made the best of a bargain

so bad for them, and prepared to defeat its ends. They installed Ignatius in most elegantly appointed apartments of a monastery, that the legates might see nothing to complain of in his treatment. To the legate - bishops themselves they gave a splendid reception, and overwhelmed them with attentions. Every condescension was now used towards the venerable Patriarch, and all the old inducements were renewed to get him to say to the legates that he had freely resigned. But the old man stood firm, and refused to share in a lie. Rodoald and Zachary began to see through things, and to hint their suspicions that all had not been fair-play in the case of Ignatius. As soon as this was perceived, the salad days of the legates were over. To lavish kindness succeeded coldness, to coldness harsh words and threats, and to threats the violent measure of deporting them from the city, one in one direction and the second in another, a hundred miles apart. Here in enforced exile, far from their country, without their accustomed comforts and without friends, those poor men were almost reduced to a state of destitution. They complained and remonstrated. It was answered that they had only themselves to blame; that if they opposed the views and wishes of the Emperor they could not look for favours at his hands; that it rested entirely with

themselves to say how long their privations should
last; they had only to intimate their willingness
to preside over a Council of Bishops, who were
already prepared to decide in favour of Photius, and
just ratify that decision in the name of the Pope,
and all their former honours, emoluments, and
luxurious comforts would be restored to them.
Crafty bribe—terrible temptation well thought out,
maturely and deliberately planned and sprung upon
them at the proper and despairing moment.   Had
they but the spirit of their Master, or a little of the
mettle of the saintly Patriarch, Church history would
never have had to stain its page with the account
of those men's disgraceful betrayal.   They shame-
fully took the bribe, and weakly fell into the temptation.   That Council was assembled, and they
presided.   As many as 300 bishops attended.
What splendid possibilities that great number of
prelates reveals for the Eastern Church had they
been of the right sort!   But that Council was
as a bench packed by Photius.   Its conclusion
was, of course, foregone.   Still Ignatius was compelled to appear.   Alone and friendless, the poor
old man confronted this formidable assemblage.
But neither Photius, in all the pomp of retinue
he loved to display, nor the presiding legates,
nor the rows on rows of those robed and bearded
prelates, nor the officials of the Imperial Court,

could weaken or intimidate a soul so upright and therefore so fearless as his :

"Thrice is he armed who hath his quarrel just."

He spoke before those men with the courage which a clear sense of right imparts, and in the language of one having authority. He arraigned the whole conduct of Photius, pointed to him as the unjust usurper of his place, and accused him of having tampered with the text of the Pope's letters in translating them from the Latin to the Greek idiom. Addressing the legates, he plainly told them he refused to believe that the Pope was a party to so unjust a proceeding. He charged them with proving false to their mission, and appealed for a hearing and for justice to the Sovereign Pontiff.

As may be imagined, he was not allowed to proceed in his address without many interruptions, and, before he had done, was forcibly removed. He was subsequently informed of the sentence of the Council. The insolent cruelty of it seems incredible. He was to present himself, not this time before the so-called Council only, but in his own cathedral, and there, before prelates and people · alike, to make public renunciation of all claims to the Patriarchate, and this under pain of degradation and imprisonment. Fearing, and rightly so, that Ignatius would never comply with this

summons of his own accord, they despatched on
the morrow a company of the Imperial Guard to
conduct him to the basilica, where they were
preparing to carry out this most humiliating ceremony of degradation. But warned of their coming
he quickly changed his robes, and, disguised as a
poor monk, he passed through the approaching
guard and escaped. For many a weary month
after this, that distinguished and saintly Patriarch
was a wanderer and fugitive from his enemies.

Meanwhile the ceremony proceeded in his absence, and Photius, with the sanction of the legates
and full Imperial approval, was installed Patriarch
of Constantinople. The sanction of the Holy See
was still wanting, but with the promised co-operation of the legates he had no doubt of quickly
securing that. The legates he now permitted to de-
part loaded with honours and costly presents. They
bore with them the Acts of the Council, adroitly
edited by Photius' own hand for presentation to
the Pope. In their company was sent the ablest
diplomatist of the Court—Leo—to influence the
Papal decision.

Now the wonder is that, with the false and
flattering tale unfolded by the returning legates,
backed by the presence of a special envoy from
the Emperor, the prudence even of a Nicholas could
have escaped deception. But it happily did. In

studying those Acts of the Council, drawn up with great formality in due canonical form, he saw at once that for some reason or other his legates had exceeded the limits of his instruction, and exercised a power with which he did not invest them. He merely wanted a report on the cause at issue—they had given a final decision. A definite sentence of deposition against the Patriarch had been pronounced and sanctioned by them. This he never intended or authorised them to do. Besides, they had brought him no personal explanation from Ignatius. There was clearly something very wrong, and notwithstanding the pleadings of Leo he refused to be moved. He summoned a council of the Western Bishops, and laid the matter before them, pointing out the suspicious circumstances of the case. They counselled him to withhold his approval of this Synod, and shared his suspicions that a wrong had been done, and an invasion of his sovereign rights had been attempted.

The result of these deliberations he embodied in an Encyclical Letter to all the Bishops of the Eastern Church. He also sent another legate, with letters for the Emperor and Photius, to Constantinople. In these he firmly informed them that further delay was necessary before he acceded to their wishes. He appealed to their loyalty to the Church to abstain from making trouble and causing a scandal, to await patiently the decision, which belonged to him by exclusive right to give, and which he would give in all justice when the time arrived, and exhorted them to receive it in the right filial spirit when given. It was well this wise Pope acted thus. The cruel feature of the whole cruel case was that the most stringent precautions had been taken by his persecutors to prevent the unfairly-deposed Patriarch from communicating with Rome. But this could not last for ever. He at length found an opportunity. A certain abbot, who had been faithful to Ignatius in all his fallen fortunes, eluded the vigilance of the ubiquitous spies, and after many privations, during a difficult and circuitous journey, succeeded in reaching Rome, and delivering his despatches to the Pope. How pleased the Holy Father must have been that prudence had so wisely guided him, when he read those letters and saw the whole villainous plot unfolded. The abbot was one witness of the story. It received further corroboration from others who, flying from persecution in the East, began now to arrive in Rome. The time for moderation and temporising was now over. The Pope resolved to throw the shield of his protecting authority over the wronged and persecuted and upright prelate. Had he thrown him over and gratified and placated the plotters of the Imperial

Court, he might have spared the Church a disastrous schism. But apart from that not being by any means a certainty, considering the restless and treacherous character of the men in question, what could the fair-minded of all time think of a ruler of the Church who abetted iniquity and consented to a sacrilegious injustice ? No, let the schism be on the head of the unrighteous. The Supreme Pastor must be above the questionable shifts of mere human policy, and stand ever and at any cost on the side of right and virtue.

Without further waiting, he cited the legates Rodoald and Zachary before a Synod. They were tried and found guilty of betraying, for bribes, the interests of the Holy See. They were deposed, degraded, and excommunicated. He sent a letter to the Emperor declaring Ignatius to be the lawful Patriarch, and the only one whom he should recognise. He maintained that Ignatius had been unlawfully and unjustly deposed, that Photius now stood in the case of a sacrilegious usurper, and as such was excommunicated, and should be publicly degraded ; and he prayed the Emperor, as he valued his salvation, to have this sentence carried out. To this an answer was composed by Photius for the Emperor, who was too young and too stupid to do it for himself. He threw off the mask, and here revealed himself in his true colours, as people

generally do when their underhand and unfair
methods are found out. His tone was most insolent and defiant. He made the Emperor claim for
himself superiority in all things, and since the
Pope did not yield to the deference and respect
the Emperor paid him, he would now, of his own
authority, confirm the appointment of Photius, and
maintain him in the See of Constantinople. Further-
more, if his Holiness continued to give him any
more trouble on the subject, *he would march on
Rome and lay it in ashes!*

Though the Pope must have anticipated some
show of temper and resistance, he was not prepared for language of this extreme nature. It was
unprecedented in a Christian monarch. Schism
he now saw to be imminent. Rather than have
it supposed he was without solicitude before so
dire a calamity, he would make one more effort for
peace. He therefore sent an Encyclical to all
the Eastern Churches, in which he made the offer
of citing both Photius and Ignatius before a Synod
in Rome, when evidence would be taken from the
witnesses of both, and all things settled legally,
fairly, and openly. This, he said, he would concede, not as admitting an appeal from his own
decision, nor as in any sense a right, but solely to
show his own earnest desire for peace in a moment
of impending crisis.

As to the Emperor, the Pope replied to him in a tone of paternal sorrow, but at the same time of unintimidated firmness. In dignified and severe words he bade him beware of raising a sacrilegious hand against God's Church; and pointed out that though the Emperor might succeed indeed in inflicting temporary injury and indignity upon it, when he had passed to judgment that Church would still survive, as it was under promise of divine protection, even against power mightier than his—the very "gates of hell"—so that his efforts should be vain, while his reckoning would be terrible and unerring.

But as well try to hold the whirlwind as the will of men embarked on wrong and desperate courses. The Bishops were forbidden to notice the offer of the Pope, and commanded to regard Photius as the lawful Patriarch. Secure now in the support of the Imperial power, he on his part assumed the independent spiritual headship of all the East. He issued Encyclical Letters to the Metropolitans and Bishops, in which he rejected the primacy of the Apostolic See, and denied that the authority of the Pope extended over the Churches of his Patriarchate. And so the Greek Schism began.

History now shows us how prophetic were the words of the Pope's warning, and that there are seasons when, men slighting the voice of His

Vicar, the great Invisible Ruler takes judgment
into His own hands. Calamities fell upon the
city of Constantinople. Destructive earthquakes
happened. Deadly pestilence broke out, and the
terrified people cried out that it was the evident
visitation of God for the unjust and wicked treatment of their saintly Patriarch.

Nor did the chief actors in this tragedy escape.
Bardas' days were numbered. A new minister had
risen to power in the State. This was Basil, a
soldier of fortune, of rude origin but of great
natural ability; he had risen to the rank of general,
and gained the admiration and confidence of the
troops. He became indispensable in the Council
of the Empire, and soon controlled it. He arraigned Bardas before the Emperor as a dissipated
squanderer of the public treasury, who brought
the nation to the verge of ruin. He had him
condemned and publicly executed. It is worthy
of note that no word was heard from Photius in
behalf of his unfortunate friend — the man to
whom he was so much beholden, his intimate
companion and his once powerful and generous
patron—not a word. He slunk away in silence
and left him to his fate. That was bad enough,
but he did a viler thing. Bardas was hardly cold
in his dishonoured grave than he addressed an
adulatory letter to the Emperor, praising his saga-

city in ridding himself and the Empire of so
dangerous a presence. He then sought favour
with his executioner, Basil, and like another statue
of Memnon, breathed a soft music of greeting and
congratulation to this rising sun. But to no avail.
He met, in turn, the fate of all mean conduct.
It was not long before the weak and wretched
Michael was done to death and Basil was Emperor.
Almost his first act was to banish Photius. Thus,
at one stroke, this man of brilliant and perverted
genius lost alike his friends and his honours, and
the bitterness of an obscure and penurious exile
was the reward of all his great ambition. It is
true that once again he regained Imperial favour.
But that was accomplished by one of the meanest
acts of his mean life. He played upon a weak-
ness of Basil. Like most men who rise from
obscurity to great eminence, the remembrance of
his origin weighed upon Basil's happiness. The
Imperial splendour would be brighter and sweeter
far to him, could he but think himself descended
from a kingly race, and not as he was—the scion
of a shepherd's hut. One day a courtier whispered
the news that the banished Photius had made a
rare discovery of an ancient manuscript, in which
the family of the Emperor was mentioned and
shown to be of an ancient, princely line in Armenia. It was a forgery, but the bait took. That

precious manuscript must be produced, and its
distinguished discoverer recalled to court. This
footing was all that Photius wanted. Once back,
his address, he knew, could gain him all he lost
once more. And the price he paid was this clever
but most barefaced forgery. However, this second
advent to place and power did not avail him very
much, for in the end his fortunes waned again, and
he died in obscurity, an obscurity so absolute that
historians have never found any traditions of its
particulars. But he had ample time in his days of
success to sow the poisoned seed of the deadly upas
tree of that schism under whose baneful shade have
languished, ever since, the once flourishing Churches
of the Orient.

   Knowing or reading this story—and it is a true
one, gathered from the most authentic sources still
existing—we may well ask was this the manner of
man who was likely to have a just or good cause
in hand? Was this the man likely to be an instrument chosen by the Most High for any special
or sacred handiwork of . His? Were his the
methods of Christ and His apostles in the kingdom of holiness and truth? Yet there are living
men in Russia and Greece to-day who own him as
the first head of their independent branches of
Christianity! Could any branch or Church be in
the way of truth with such a founder?

These questions have a serious bearing—nay, a vital interest for those they concern—for they touch not merely a matter of curious history or mere temporal or worldly dispute. They involve for many that question of the last importance—the eternal safety. Nor is it by any means to be supposed that the Easterns have always remained indifferent or rested content with their separation from the parent Church. They have been very uneasy about it. Since the time of Photius three attempts have been made at reconciliation. The first after the second and final banishment of this unhappy intriguer; the second at the Council of Lyons, in 1274; and the third in Florence in 1439. Then the Empire went down before the power of the Turks, and the city of Constantine, for its sins, passed under that fell dominion up to this our day. From time to time many, especially among the educated Russians, have individually rejoined the Roman Communion. Not very long ago a member of the distinguished and noble family of the Schouvaloffs became a Catholic priest. He has published the story of his conversion. Listen to his sentiments about the Russian-Greek Church :—

"If circumstances have not permitted me to serve my country by fighting for her, let my prayer—let my life, if need be—be henceforth consecrated to her, and let me bring, if only a

grain of sand, to the edifice of its spiritual re-
generation. . . . The Russian Church is being
undermined daily more and more by Rationalism,
the gangrene of the upper classes, and by heresies
among the people. She will doubtless triumph
over error, but only when in the bosom of unity,
when she is reconciled with the infallible authority
of that august tribunal which began in the supper
chamber at Jerusalem, and still sits in St. Peter's
at Rome " (" My Conversion and Vocation," by
Father Schouvaloff, Barnabite).

Thirty years ago now, this Count Schouvaloff,
soon after his ordination as a Catholic priest,
founded an Association of Prayer for the return
of the Russian Church to unity with the See of
St. Peter. The late Pope, Pius IX., took a great
interest in this Association. In his Brief of Confirmation, dated September 2, 1862, he said:
" Especially ever since we have sat in St. Peter's
chair, we have desired and prayed to God for
nothing more earnestly than that the Christians
of the entire world may join in communion with
this Holy See, which is the centre of unity."
When these words were written, no one dreamed
that the Czar would ever send an ambassador to
dwell near the Vatican. And yet the unexpected
has come to pass. Such is the force of earnest
prayer.

PART III

THE PROTESTANT DEFECTION

I.—PREDISPOSING CAUSES

WE must now change the scene from Constantinople in the ninth century, to the heart of Europe, about six hundred years afterwards—to inquire how it has happened that Prussia, part of the German States, Norway, Sweden, Denmark, Holland, part of the Swiss Republic, and Great Britain, have come to be known as Protestant countries in contra-distinction to Italy, Austria, Hungary, Poland, a third of the German States, a third of Switzerland, Belgium, France, Spain, Portugal, and Ireland, recognised as Catholic countries.

When we remember the indisputable fact of history, that up to the sixteenth century all these countries were Catholic only, it becomes a question of absorbing interest to inquire what could have caused so sudden and wide a parting of the nations on the vital subject of religion as to make them henceforth diametrically opposed.

It can be easily seen how helpful to many a

plain and candid statement of the causes leading
to this deplorable disunion may be. These causes,
honestly set forth, without partiality or intention
of offence, merely as a matter of history, cannot but
make for reunion among earnest and serious minds.
It is our intention thus to set forth those causes.

No great or violent change in human affairs ever
comes about quite of a sudden. A long course and
concurrence of events generally lead up to it. It
was so with the great religious change known as
Protestantism.

It is not an easy thing for us, in the midst of this
magically-changed world of the nineteenth century,
to cast our minds backwards four or five hundred
years, and duly appreciate the frame of men's manners in these distant and different days. So that
in encountering things that to us seem strange and
little edifying, the French epigram, *Autres temps,
autres meurs*, will be useful as a modifying agent.

For a good while before the sixteenth century it
is universally admitted that a great deal of reformation in matters of discipline was sadly needed in
the Church :—

1. Certain members of the stricter observance of
the Franciscan Order, professing to be shocked by
the too great luxury which prevailed at the time,
formed themselves into a kind of indignation society.
They assumed the name of Fraticelli. They be-

came the terror, and also the nuisance of Europe. They went about denouncing Bishops, and even those in higher places, both in the Church and State. Their descriptions and denunciations excited and unsettled the people. They weakened respect for the ministers of religion, and so injured its practice. They sowed in the popular mind a contempt for all authority, besides restless discontent, a fifteenth-century Socialism, in fact, which ran into frightful and disorderly licence in the end. These Fraticelli well-nigh upturned all society in Europe before they were finally suppressed by the authority of the Pope. As may be supposed, all this predisposed the minds of many for religious revolt.

2. There was a long season of miserable faction-wars, especially in Italy, in which the Popes more than once became involved. Through the violent disturbance in political affairs they were obliged to leave Rome altogether, and for sixty-nine years resided at Avignon, in France. Part of this was a sad, scandalous time. There were contentions about the Papal elections between the Cardinals in Italy and the Cardinals in France. There came a season when as many as three Popes were reigning simultaneously, and the faithful knew not which was the right one ; their allegiance was divided, and schism afflicted the Church. All this misery tended to weaken the authority of the Sovereign Pontiffs,

and respect for their high office and sacred dignity
suffered decline.

3. When at length, at the close of the fifteenth
century, the seat of government was re-established
in Rome, the Papal dignity became the prize of
contention for noble and powerful families. Men
were elected to that sacred office whose actions left
room to think that it had become the vulgar prey
of worldly ambition. Some of them, members of
the nobility, surrounded it with a splendour and
worldly pomp that scandalised the poor and the
simple-minded. Others had not the cleanest re-
cords from their earlier life, though it has now been
established that not one of them *while Pope* com-
promised in any way the moral rectitude of the
Papacy, much less betrayed or tampered, in any
particular, with the sacred deposit of doctrine. The
worst case brought forward, that of Alexander VI., of
the Borgian family, has now been shown, especially by
Jungmann, in his Dissertations on Church History,
to have been much and maliciously exaggerated. It
is to be remembered that he was sixty-one years old
at his election—the sober and mellow time of life—
and whatever his younger years may have been, he
made on the whole a good Pope. It is the pitch
of some really bad lay members of his family, to
whom he was, perhaps, naturally too indulgent, that
has fastened on the memory of this Pontiff some-

what unfairly. The richest princely family of Italy,
at this time, was, perhaps, the Medici. Lorenzo,
its founder, was surnamed the Magnificent. It
was their ambition to see some of its members sit
on the Pontifical throne, and it was the Medici
Popes, chiefly, that drew the eyes of a censorious
and censuring world on the wealth and magnificence
of the Papal Court, and their liberal and lavish
patronage of the neo-pagan art and literature.

4. It was at this period, too, that the Dominican
friar, Savonarola, was bestirring himself with a well-
meaning but undisciplined zeal. Italy resounded
with his denunciations of luxury in high places.
He spared neither Pope nor Cardinal nor Bishop.
He fell foul of the all-powerful family of the Medici,
and it was through them principally that his tragic
and dreadful end was brought about. It has now
come to light that Alexander VI. wished to save
him. But the Medici would not let him leave
Florence, and he suffered in the public square his
death of strangulation and burning. Both his undisciplined zeal and his unhappy death left their
mark of mischief on the times.

5. Then came what is known, and, I think,
wrongly known, as the Revival of Learning. It
had better be named, rather, the substitution of
one learning for another. Learning was not in
abeyance, as the former title would suppose. Only

it was of a different kind, and many good judges
claim to be permitted to think, of a better and
more salutary kind. Was there no learning displayed in the monumental works of St. Thomas?
Were St. Bonaventure, or Bernard of Clairvaux, or
Pope Innocent III. very uninstructed and ignorant
persons? What was the learning to be "revived"
that could add much to the penetrating and almost
universal wisdom to be yet found in the literary
labours of these and many others that might be
mentioned in these pre-fifteenth-century times?

 To believe these literary revivalists, the scholastic
studies of the Christian ages had destroyed all taste
and elegance in letters. To expose this wretched
falsehood, I here dare to place side by side the
most ornate and studied of Horace's odes and an
ode to St. John the Baptist, composed by a monk,
in the same metre, five hundred years before this
so-called revival—and let scholars judge :—

ODE XII. AD AUGUSTUM.

Quem virum aut heroa, lyra, vel acri
Tibia sumes celebrare Clio
Quem Deum? cujus resonet jocosa
       Numen imago.

Aut in umbrosis Heliconis oris
Aut super Pindo gelidove in Hieme
Unde vocalem temere insecutæ
       Orphea sylvæ.

Arte materna rapidos morantem
Fluminum lapsus celeresque ventos
Blandum et auritas fidebus canoris
        Ducere quercus.

Quid prius dicam solitis parentis
Laudibus? qui res hominum et Decorum
Qui mare et terras, variisque mundum
        Temporat horis.

Romulum post hos prius an quietum
Pompili regnum memorem an superbos
Tarquini fasces dubito an Catonis
        Nobili lethum.

Regulum et Scauros animæque magmæ
Prodigum Paulum superante Pœno
Gratus insigni referam Camœna
        Fabriciumque.

.   .   .   .   .   .

Te minor latum reget æquus orbem
Tu gravi curru quaties olympum
Tu parum castis inimica mittes
        Fulmina lucis.

ODE AD JOANNEM.

Ut queant laxis resonare fibris
Mira gestorum famuli tuorum
Solve polluti labii reatum
        Sancte Joannes.

Nuntius celso veniens olympo
Te patri magnum fore nasciturum
Nomen et vitæ seriem gerendœ
        Ordine promit.

Ille promissi dubius superni
Perdidit promptæ modulos loquelæ
Sed reformasti genitus peremptæ
        Organa vocis.

Ventris obstruso recubans cubili
Senseras Regem thalamo manentem
Hinc parens nati meritis uterque
        Abdita pandit.

Antra deserti teneris sub annis
Civium turmas fugiens petisti
Ne levi posses maculare vitam
        Crimine linguæ.

Præbuit durum tegumen camelus
Artubus sacris, strophium bidentes
Cui latex haustum sociata pastum
        Mella locustis.

Ceteri tantum cecinere Vatum
Corde præsago jubar affuturum
Tu quidem mundi scelus auferentem
        Indice prodis.

Non fuit vasti spatium per orbis
Sanctior quisquam genitus Joanne
Qui nefas sæcli meruit lavantem
        Tingere lymphis.

I might also quote St. Thomas' hymns to the Eucharist, and the beautiful *Stabat Mater* and *Dies iræ* of Innocent III.

The learning to be revived, it appeared, was the pagan classics—the beauties of Greek and Latin prose and poetry. And this revival had a marked and dissolvent effect on manners, and a debilitating effect on Christian dogma.

With pagan literature pagan art was also brought back, and with still more dangerous consequences. The literature and art of an age mutually reflect each other. In a time of pure and spiritual literature you find a pure and moralising art. Hitherto Christian art was inspired by Christian dogma and Christian morality. It sought not to please, or pander to men's evil propensities. That it was not without high merit, and that a good deal of it was of undying excellence, any connoisseur can tell. But still it palled on the evil disposed, and these gladly welcomed the return of an art which pandered to sensuality.

6. At this time, too, as a natural consequence of the accumulated piety of fifteen centuries, many churches and monasteries were most richly endowed. It is a maxim, delivered by the highest authority, that many possessions and spiritual perfection do not go usually hand in hand. It is not surprising then, however deplorable, to find that this spiritual perfection was sadly on the decline in institutions where it most should flourish.

The "new-learning men" eagerly fastened on the weakest of spots in Church life. They affected a venomous hatred of scholasticism. It kept them so long and tyrannously out of their glorious

E

inheritance of pagan enlightenment. And were not
the monasteries the nurseries of scholasticism? So
they turned a fierce light on the idleness and fine
living of the monks. They opened a raking fire on
their "lazy ignorance and crafty superstitions"—
stupidly ungrateful thing of these gentry, newly
polished with pagan veneer, to do; for if those
same monks or their brethren had not laboriously
copied out the works of the pagan authors and
handed them down through ages, where would your
"revivers of learning" be then? The leader in
this attack on the monks and scholastic monasticism,
or monastic scholasticism, whichever he called it, and
the man who did most to influence the educated
minds of nearly all Europe, and predispose them
to unyoke from their allegiance to the Church, and
gave, moreover, most plausible pretext for the coming
cry of Reformation, deserves a special notice.

7. Erasmus was a great power in his day, and
greater even since his day. It was unfortunate for
the Church and for the faith that he was so. He
was an *enragé* of the " new learning," and became
a scholar of European fame. He stands in the
invidious light of a favoured child, turning ungrate-
fully and ungraciously on his mother, for he was a
priest, and, like Luther, one of the Austin Friars.
On his own confession he never should have been
one. The calling was imposed upon him before

his judgment was ripe. Still, he owed his training and the development of his rare talents to Church-men. His youth was overshadowed, and left the mark of a great sorrow on his life. When this happens to men of genius, it often finds vent and relief in *persiflage*, and bitter attacks against those whom they deem its cause. Erasmus seemed to find a savage and lifelong delight in avenging himself on the clerical career and all its votaries and doings, for having been unwittingly cramped and bound up with it when young. His illegitimate birth, too, left a pang which developed that morbid sensitiveness so dangerous in great minds. His father, on the death of his mistress, in penance, became a priest, and destined this unhappy fruit of his unblessed passion to be a co-victim in the repentant sacrifice. Was ever a man so fated? When power of reflection and self-consciousness came to him, he resented bitterly his hard fate. But it was too late. He had taken the irrevocable orders, and in addition had deliberately uttered the three self-immolating vows of religion. Still the hold of conscience was strong upon him. He never married. But he studied to make the cruel situa-tion as tolerable to himself as possible. Without any observable scandal he soon managed to escape from the restrictions of the conventual life. A complacent Bishop in France gave him shelter and

support in the sinecure of a secretaryship. Of a
delicate and suffering constitution, the comforts of
his new position were a mercy to him. It made
it possible for him to give himself to his favourite
studies, of which he was ardently fond. He could
write Latin and compose Greek like an ancient
classic author. He caught up again, besides, the old
elegance of diction and distinction of style, which
he and his friends declared to have been lost in the
heaped-up rubbish of scholasticism.

Later on he goes to Paris. It was less com-
fortable and more ill-smelling than the Paris we
know, but was then, as now, one of the greater
literary centres. He was worldly-wise, you see, as
well as greatly gifted. Here, though things did
not smile for him, he managed to publish the first
fruits of his studies—first his "Adages," and then
the book that made his fame, "In Praise of Folly."
This work was hailed with delight by all the "new-
learning" men. It was the swiftest and sharpest
shaft ever shot against the old enemy, the scho-
lastics. Erasmus was the lion of the hour. Flattering congratulations and liberal offers poured in from
every side. He was invited to Rome by the patrons,
in that city, of the classic revival. It is even said
that hopes were held out to him of a Cardinal's hat.
But flattering as the invitation was, he did not
accept it. While in Paris he gained his living by

tutoring two sons of an English nobleman, Lord
Mountjoy. With the elder he formed a close and
lasting friendship. When he came to his title he
proved a generous patron to Erasmus. It was on his
pension, in fact, that Erasmus lived for the rest of his
life. He went to England on a visit to his noble
friend. This was his second visit to that country.
He had gone before he had published this famous
book, in the company of his pupil. On that occasion
he had been presented at Court. Prince Hal was
then a lad, rather fond of study, and took a fancy
to the scholarly Dutchman, and even corresponded
with him for some time. He also met Sir Thomas
More, on whom he exercised a sort of fascinating
attractiveness too, for that great and saintly man
remained long his friend.

On this second visit Henry was king, the eighth
of that name, and it is worth while remarking that
this time he cut Master Erasmus dead. Still a
fervent Catholic, he was perspicacious enough to
see through the ribaldry of the great book of the
hour. Its vile onslaught on his friends the monastic fathers was little to his taste. His powerful
minister, Cardinal Wolsey, never took to Erasmus
either. Nevertheless he had a flattering reception
from the universities. He had an offer of a Greek
lectureship from Cambridge. It is in strange con-
tradiction of himself, that though these English

seats of learning were at that time entirely in the hands of the religious orders—Franciscans, Augustinians, and Benedictines—Erasmus should have left on record a most eloquent tribute to the scholarly efficiency and advancement in learning and mental culture he found there. But so it is. The Archbishop of Canterbury—Warham—was very kind to him, and even conferred a benefice on him. This, however, he never filled, for soon after, most likely through the action of Cardinal Wolsey, he had to leave England, and he never again returned.

His "Praise of Folly" was followed by other works, composed in the retreat of his native marshes of Holland. They all breathed the same destroying sarcasm and criticism of things once revered and held holy in the popular mind, so that it can be truly said that no other one man did more to prepare the way, especially among the educated classes of the time, for the fatal religious rent in Europe than Desiderius Erasmus. To his malign genius must be attributed, and at his door must be laid, that profound hatred of monastic institutions in every form that has characterised Protestantism ever since.

It seems strange to us that he never incurred the censure of the Church, while to non-Catholics it must appear as one instance, at least, of extreme toleration.

Nor did he ever leave the Church's communion.

On the contrary, he viewed with alarmed dis-
approval the lengths to which his rougher brethren
across the borders in Germany permitted themselves to go. The coarse ravings of Luther, Beza,
and Zwingle he held in special horror, and even
used his eloquent pen in reproval of their excesses.
But it was too late. He had contributed his guilty
share to the *débâcle* beyond recall. As well might
the little wanton boy who opens the floodgates of
a dam, sit crying on the bank because he cannot
call back the devastating waters.

His end, in the eyes of those who value the last
sacraments, was sad and dreadful enough. In the
winter of his days, and the winter of his icy land,
he flitted on a southward journey in search of a
summer clime. He got as far as Bâle, by the fast-
flowing Rhine, when a fatal illness seized him.
Now it happened that owing to the progress of the
religious revolt which he did so much to foment,
the Catholic religion had just been interdicted in
that town, and there was not a priest to be found
within its precincts. So he died vainly asking for
one, and died without the rites of the dying, and
was buried without those of the dead—like many
another, as he sowed so did he reap.

Thus these various causes spread abroad a spirit
of discontent and unrest, which too successfully
predisposed many to rally to the call for separation

from the ancient Church, made under the specious
name of Reformation.

To reassure any who may regard the foregoing
statements as admissions too freely made, it is only
necessary to recall the principle that scandals and
frailties and self-indulgence are not to be found
inculcated anywhere in the Church's teaching, nor
in the Rules and Constitutions of Monastic Life.
They are, therefore, when found, to be attributed to
the defects of fallen nature, the individual neglect
of divine grace, and abuse of individual free-will.

We shall now examine the immediate causes
which led to this great disunion in the different
countries.

II.—GERMANY.

As might be expected from the youngest branch of the
Holy Roman Empire, Germany was the most Catholic of countries up to the beginning of the sixteenth
century.   The brief account of its sudden defection
from the Church in non-Catholic school-books is
something like this: The Pope was building a great
cathedral in Rome, and being short of funds he
sent a Dominican friar, one Tetzel, to sell indulgences to raise the money.   This so shocked the
piety and stirred the soul of a certain great and
gifted man, named Martin Luther, that he raised an

outcry against the impious proceeding; and finding, as he went further in his investigations, that
there were many things more wrong in the state
of Rome even than selling indulgences, he preached
an eloquent crusade against the Pope and the
Papacy, and saved his country from its crafty de-
lusions, superstitions, and corruptions. Oh, how
many millions of minds have been fed on this
plausible tale any time these three hundred years
—how many are still being fed at this hour? The
young take the schoolroom lesson as settling the
matter for ever, and seldom afterwards in the busy
whirl of life care to recur to irksome memories and
open an investigation for themselves. Their Protestantism has been settled for them long ago, and
they hug it as a thing recommended to them by
every one they revered in childhood.

We must interrogate a little more closely the
chief actor and witness in this affair. It cannot
in the least be objectionable to do so, because, since
he put himself so forward and made such a disturbance in things that concerned so many others as
well as himself, his life and character became public
property, and ought to be carefully examined. It
is not usually mentioned in the popular account
that Martin Luther was a Catholic priest. But he
was. He was a priest, moreover, of the Augus-
tinian Order, better known to English people as the

Austin Friars—as that place in London is still so
called, where stood one of their old monasteries—
which meant, that in addition to priest's orders,
he had taken the three vows of religion : poverty,
chastity, and obedience, which he solemnly promised God to observe to the end of his days, for
the sake of the hundred-fold and the life eternal.
And when his story is done, I think you will agree,
it had been far better for himself had he never left
the labourer's cottage near the mines of Eisleben,
where his father honestly toiled for the support of
his family, and not taken upon himself these grave
obligations.   Ten years he had been a priest before
Friar Tetzel ever came to preach in Saxony.   Part
of the time he had been an exact and scrupulous,
indeed over-scrupulous, novice.   Like Erasmus, he
then began to find that this manner of life was little
to his taste, but unlike him it was entirely of his
own seeking.   So anxious was he to advance in his
studies that at one time he took to playing the flute
in the streets to get means to continue them.   He
won the sympathy of a musical benefactress who
befriended him, and he went on with his schooling
at Erfurt.   It was in a panic of fright that the idea
of entering religion came to him.   A companion was
struck dead by lightning at his side, and he fled
the world to prepare for the great uncertain certainty.   The Fathers of the convent, recognising a

strong rugged talent in him, gave him every facility
for study. He did them credit. He took his philo-
sophy degree at Erfurt, and then was sent to
Wittenberg University to take that of divinity,
which he did with great honour. He was promoted
to a professorship, and was looked on as one of the
most brilliant and promising members of his Order.
None could know him better than the brethren with
whom he had to live under a common rule. The
sketch they have given of him is something like
this : His external appearance was heavy and coarse.
It was a good index to his mental qualities—stub-
born and obstinate, will-strong, passionate—a sturdy
comprehensive intellect, too rugged to be brilliant
or attractingly refined— dark and gloomy humours,
alternating with boisterous mirth—a morbid and
sensitive pride, intensified by a strong self-reliant
character—he was capable of close application—
he had eloquence of the loud-resounding, rather
than of the winning and cultured kind—and an
appetite not easily appeased, especially for the
national beverage. His piety, on which they do
not greatly remark, was chiefly exhibited in those
painful paroxysms of scruples, or rather, in his
case, for he owned to frequent falls from his
strong passions, the writhings of remorse. He
soon wearied of the struggle and tired of the constant recourse he was obliged to have to the trying

spiritual remedies of the religious life. He was teaching theology, so he invented, in the form of a thesis, a theory to meet his own conscience, and set his mind at rest about his sinful inclinations and his unhappy consent to lustful indulgences. For certain conditions of the mind, and under the promptings of nature, he established an impeccability, and all such frailties as could not command our sorrow or atonement the merits of Christ were sufficient to cover. Here was the first foreshadowing of the celebrated doctrine of justification by imputation, as distinguished from the co-operation with Christ's merits by personal works on our part. This has ever since been the pivot of the whole Protestant question. We have seen pretty plainly why Father Martin Luther invented it, and there is no novice so young in the spiritual life who would not tell you that it was a mean and cowardly subterfuge. "Yes, but he supported his contention by Scripture authority, especially from texts in St. Paul." Shakspeare was wiser than you, even in the very early non-Catholic times in England :—

> "There is no damnèd error
> But men will bless and prove it with a text."

Father Luther was a unit among thousands in Church authority, and ninety-nine per cent., not only of that age, but of the fifteen previous ages, were against his interpretation of these difficult and isolated passages of Scripture—think of that. No ; he wanted an excuse for his freer enjoyment, and to give himself courage to use it he persuaded as many as possible to avail themselves of it too. Believe me, you have a great deal of the pretext for Reformation shut up in that little fact in Father Martin's earlier career. This thesis being something hitherto undiscussed, indeed unheard of, not much comment was made on it at first, as happens when a surprise is sprung on people. But some complaint was already made about it. Then came the preaching of the indulgences for St. Peter's. This he made his opportunity to come forward in all his impatience of disciplinary restraint and defiance of Church authority.

Now, it is really too much to ask any instructed and intelligently - reflective man to believe that Father Martin Luther was scandalised at the publication of indulgences. That would have been a piece of pure affectation on his part.

Will any one tell me that this Doctor of Divinity, who won his degree so brilliantly—this man who was teaching Catholic theology for seven years— did not know the meaning of indulgences ? that according to the Church's explanation of them there could possibly be no room for scandal unless a

mercy and a consoling concession could be scandalous; that they are founded on the "loosing and
binding" power as plainly imparted by Our Lord—
a power much less than that of forgiving sin,
which Luther never called in question—and that
the salutary practice on the part of the Church of
granting these indulgences and of gaining them
on the part of the faithful prevailed from earliest
Christian times? Of course he did. Otherwise he
would not be fit to be either a doctor or professor.
That line in Shakspeare hits off the case:—

"Methinks the gentleman did protest too much."

There was great enthusiasm about erecting this
great Basilica in memory of the Prince of the
Apostles. It was to be without a rival (as it is
at this present moment) amid the temples of the
world. It was a supreme effort to give to God's
glory and worship all that was best in human genius
and skill, and in art and wealth of material. There
was a natural anxiety to get all Christians to contribute to the vast cost contemplated, and they were
now permitted to contribute to this purpose instead
of giving an alms to the poor as one of the conditions of gaining an indulgence. If Luther or
anybody else had noticed any fault in the method
of collecting the alms, no one would blame them
for sending a complaint and a remonstrance to the

proper quarter and trying to have the thing quietly remedied. And if Luther had been a really good and gently-disposed man, as every edifying religious man ought to be, that is the course he would have pursued. But no, he raised a storm and a tempest. If dust lies about the crevices and corners of your house, and you let in a whirlwind instead of using a feather brush, you would be held guilty of the unwisest of folly in laying the edifice in ruins to get at the dust. We all know that a good deal of secular dust can gather about the nooks and cornices of the Church from the frailty of its human elements, but it was not a feather brush that Friar Luther handled to clean it out. He thought it better to pull it all down, which he proceeded to do in a very violent fashion, and he certainly succeeded in taking a big slice out of it before he had done. No one was more taken aback by his turbulent clamour than poor Father Tetzel, the preacher of the indulgences. Such accusations were quite unlooked for by him. They had such an effect on him that he went home and died of chagrin. But before doing so he left a very telling and able vindication of himself in all these proceedings. From this it would appear that we have been granting too much about the alleged abuses. The truth is, there was something far other than indulgences troubling this Luther's perturbed soul, and we think we have pretty accurately put our finger on the weak spot. He was a poor unhappy priest, who made a mistake, and thought he could best escape from the situation by breaking it up. He could gain a little public *éclat* and celebrity to boot. It was much nicer to be a popular hero, admired for a bold and undaunted genius, than a poor friar unfrocked for breaking his vows. It was not yesterday or to-day he had known Catherine Bora when he led her to the altar of sacrilege. It was some time since he troubled the quiet of her cloister, and that kind of intimacy of a priest with a nun the Canon Law proclaims the greatest of crimes, and visits with the severest of penalties. Father Martin's story is a curious and interesting bit of soul-study.

But surely, you will say, a nation's faith could not be so suddenly changed by the action of an individual. True, neither Luther nor any one man could do that without many concurrent causes to aid. Many of these I have already pointed out, as far as the people at large went. Their temporal rulers—kings, kinglets, princes, dukes, and barons—saw in this movement against supreme Church authority a rare chance of freeing themselves from a yoke which many a time made itself chafingly felt in the interests of morality and popular rights. The memories of Canossa, of Philip the Fair, of the

English John, and of German Henry were ever before them. As long as they remained children of
the Church, as they all were, or had to be out-
wardly up to this moment, part of their religion
was to recognise the spiritual fatherhood of the
Pope. His paternal eye passed their conduct in
review, and to his reproving voice they could not
be inattentive. It was so for a thousand years.
Freed from this restraint, which beyond doubt had
been, on the whole, most salutary for society and
for the Christian world, it could not but result that
fuller power should fall into their hands, rendering
their rule purely absolute and irresponsible. It was
little wonder then that some of those ruling princes
secretly rejoiced at this religious upheaval, and as
soon as it was safe, accorded it belligerent rights,
then became its allies, and finally its patrons and
protectors. It was a splendid and a tempting prize
for them. But the poor, short-sighted multitude
little dreamed that it was a rivet the more in the
chain of their bondage. It was only later they
keenly felt that the Papal brake was off the chariot
of despotism. For this and other reasons, Luther
had a most willing and powerful abetter in
Frederick, the Prince Elector of Saxony. He
had been an especial favourite of that ruler.
Frederick was the founder of the Wittenberg University, and he thought that Luther had brightened

F

its dawn by his talent and eloquence. He was grateful to him. In social hours he was the favoured guest at the stronghold castle amid the Saxon hills. He was a jovial boon companion in the hours of high wassail. His tales and jokes, which were unrestrained by any rules of nice taste or refinement, kept the princely table in wild but coarse delight. In the days of pursuit, when the Imperial hand sought him for disturbing the public peace, its portcullis was lowered to take him into a safe retreat. When the sky grew serener he sallied out again and carried his impetuous propaganda far and wide through the German States. Thus through Frederick and Luther the revolt against the ancient Church took root and spread in Germany.

The civil rulers delightedly found another piece of good luck in these disturbances. With the disestablishment of the old Church came, of course, the disendowment of its richly-left institutions, and many a royal and ducal coffer depleted in lawless wars was then suddenly and most agreeably refilled with their spoils. It was mammon joining the world in the struggle, and every one knows what a powerful combination that is. And when you add to this the spirit within us all, that hungers for the easy and the flowery way, it will be seen that the new system which held a gate ajar to

such a path, had everything on its side with which
to win.

The Duchy of Brandenburg had long been ruled
by the military religious order of the Teutonic
Knights. This was the remnant of those remarkable
military bodies which were the unique fruit of the
ages of Faith and the Crusades. The flower of
the chivalry of Europe was enrolled in its ranks,
and scarcely a noble family but had a member
among the famous knights. They were laymen
and yet religious, and to the three ordinary vows
added a fourth, of fighting in defence of Christendom against the dreaded and threatening Turk.
Twenty thousand lances often marched in fulfilment
of that vow, and the paynim soil ofttimes shook
beneath the tread of this formidable cavalry. The
most celebrated of them were the Knights of St.
John of Jerusalem and the Templars, both suppressed before this time, having outlived their
utility and seen their days of decay. Albert of
Brandenburg was the religious commandant of the
Teutonic Knights in the opening of the sixteenth
century. In 1522 he astonished Germany and
grieved his friends, by deserting his Order and
marrying a Danish princess. His object was to
secularise the possessions of the monastery and
inaugurate civil government. He disbanded his
religious subjects, and offered them wives and

official employment. This was the foundation of the Prussian monarchy, and therefore of the present Imperial German dynasty.

Albert thus broke, of course, definitely with the Pope, and Luther was not slow to angle for so considerable and desirable an adherent. He sent one of his henchmen named Osiander into Brandenburg to treat with Albert. The negotiations ended in a request for Lutheran preachers to instruct the people in the new and easier creed, and supersede the Catholic religion. It was thus that Prussia became Protestant.

The most powerful of the Duchies of North Germany in those days was Hesse, now Hesse-Darmstadt. Its ruler was the Elector Philip, a perfect type of the rude and unruly swashbuckler German baron of the novel. There were many reasons, private as well as of State, why he should welcome a chance to defect from the Papal authority. His matrimonial exploits were of a kind to meet only short shrift in that direction. A monk who performed his own marriage would not be so particular. Nor was he. So Duke Philip was won to Luther's side. He opened his territory to three apostate friars—Lambert a Franciscan, Melander a Dominican, and Lenning a Carthusian—to preach Lutheranism, and so Hesse became Protestant.

These were the beginnings and the seed of all

German Protestantism. The candid inquirer may well ask himself here, is this a safe or reputable spiritual enterprise in which to be deeply involved when the Master of the House comes to see who watcheth?

III.—OTHER COUNTRIES

SWEDEN was Catholic from the ninth century to the year 1540. A little before the latter date two brothers—Nicholas and Lawrence Petri—had returned to their country, having finished their studies in the University of Wittenberg. They there imbibed the spirit of the Lutheran movement, and ardently advocated it among their fellow-countrymen. With the influence of a good family name, and the spell of reputed scholarship where scholarship was rare, they succeeded marvellously in undermining all Church authority, and vindicating independent and private judgment. Four years after their propaganda had begun, Gustave Ericson was elected king in reward for his successful rebellion against the Danes, who had long dominated the Scandinavian Bund. It suited a new and poor ruler of a country impoverished by a protracted and sanguinary struggle to side with those demanding the abolition of the ancient Church. It was a Church rich with the endowments of seven hundred years. With relentless cruelty and rapacity he swept them all into his coffers. He declared himself and his kingdom Lutheran, and murdered and exiled all who resisted or refused to conform.

Thus her first king, tempted by gold, led Sweden into Protestantism.

DENMARK may be reckoned as Christian and Catholic from the baptism of Harold Klak in 826 to Christian III. in 1539. It was this latter monarch who received the innovations of the so-called Reformers, and for a reason identical with that of his conqueror in Sweden. The half-century of international struggle in Scandinavia under his predecessors had left the Danish exchequer very empty indeed. He permitted many Lutheran preachers to harangue the multitude against the old order of religion, and when the time was ripe, confiscated its many possessions. Lutheranism became the State religion, and still remains so.

NORWAY was under Danish rule until 1813. This explains her form of faith.

HOLLAND'S separation from Catholic unity does not belong to this time. It did not take place until nearly a hundred years later, and then it was more in hatred of the Spanish, whose rule the Netherlanders overthrew, than anything else. This political motive for religious change may account for the fact that out of three million in-

habitants in that prosperous little country, there
are still over one million Catholics.

SWITZERLAND—the mountain-home of Tell and
ancient freedom—the land of the Helvetian warriors
who stayed the Roman legions in their victorious
marches—was Christian and Catholic from a much
earlier period than the preceding countries. But it
did not escape the separation contagion of the sixteenth century. The history of the seceding Cantons
is singularly like that of Saxony. Here, too, you
have an unhappy priest dissatisfied with his state,
only Zwingle was not a friar like Luther. He
was an ordinary parish priest—a man of bold and
determined character rather than talented or very
learned. You will seek in vain for any one who
has a good word to say of Zwingle. All admit
he was a bad, even a depraved man, and the
opinion is based on his own shameless confession
of loose and reckless morals. He, and a few
more priests like himself, petitioned the governing
authorities to legalise sacerdotal marriage, professing their inability to live continently. When the
Franciscans came into these regions to collect for
St. Peter's, it is not surprising that Zwingle and
his friends, taking a leaf out of Luther's book,
violently opposed them, and finally obliged them
to retire from the country. Zwingle was a friend
of the Syndic or Mayor of Tuguria, of which he

was pastor. With his co-operation and that of the bad priests he called around him, of whom the penman was Œcolampadius, a religious of the Order of St. Birgitta, Zwingle commenced his crusade against the Papal authority. The northern and western cantons, bordering on Germany, all fell away; but the southern, near the Italian borders, remained Catholic. From this came one of these miserable internecine wars of race. In the final battle of Capell, which the Catholics gained, Zwingle was slain in the thick of the fight. But it is doubtful whether Protestantism would have got any firm footing in the country—its sponsors were so disreputable—had there not appeared in Geneva a Frenchman named Calvin, who fled from his country to avoid an impeachment for heresy. He was not a priest, but was studying in a French seminary, such as seminaries went in these pre-Tridentine days, for the purpose of being one, when he became suspected of favouring the new German doctrines. The French, warned by the sanguinary results of Protestantism in many parts of Germany, were determined to keep their borders free from so disturbing an element, and Calvin had to flee. He settled in Geneva, where he found freer scope for his religious fancies. Here he published his curious book, in four volumes, called, "The Christian Institutions." It was nothing but a medley of various

unauthorised modern doctrinal speculations found in
the writings of Luther, Œcolampadius, and Melancthon. A man of brooding and earnest spirit, he soon
became a kind of Pope to the new Swiss Protestants.
Later on he found the means to introduce his views
in a portion of his native land, where his followers
afterwards became known by the name of Hugue-
nots—a word of extremely obscure origin—probably
a French nickname.

There are not many Scotchmen, perhaps, aware
that their religion is Swiss Calvinism. But so
it is. It came about in this way : When Calvin
was throning it in Geneva, an ex-Scottish priest,
named John Knox, came to pay him a visit.
From so simple a thing as this the religion of
almost a whole race took shape. It was the
doctrine he imbibed at the feet of this modern
but perverted Gamaliel which he imported and
propagated in bonny Scotland. It will be necessary to see what fate led him to Geneva. This
Knox was of very obscure parentage, and, as a
kind of poor scholar, received an education at the
Catholic University of St. Andrews. Not very
much is known of him for some time after
this, but he was a priest when Mary of Lor-
raine was Queen, in 1530. While engaged in
teaching somewhere in his native Haddington,
he met a certain Father George Wishart, and by

that magnetism which forcibly attracts similar characters to each other, a close intimacy sprang up between them. This Wishart had returned from a tour in Germany, where he had lived in the full tide of the religious controversies and change then going on in that country. He returned full of the news, and deeply imbued with the novelties. In character he was moody, speculative, restless, and discontented, and, as his figure and hard features indicated, of dark and fierce temper, capable of extreme fanaticism and pitiless measures. Knox was the replica of Wishart. When one is described, we have the picture of the other. And these two distortions of our better nature loved each other — as distortions sometimes do. Wishart, after his German experiences, soon threw off the allegiance and the yoke of the Catholic priesthood, of which he was no great ornament, and, with Knox for a henchman, he set out to play the Luther of Scotland. It is told that when he came to a town or village to preach, John Knox always preceded him with grim and stern visage, holding aloft a two-handed sword. This little sketch lets in a good deal of light on these ex-Catholic priests and their doings. However, things were not ripe for a Luther just yet in Scotland, so Wishart was laid by the heels, and imprisoned on the charge of heresy against the Church and treason against the State. John ran away, or, as he puts it, Wishart advised his reserving himself to work in a better day. Wishart was brought to trial, condemned, and burned on the square of St. Andrews. Ah! These were cruel days, and, in some respects, as unwise as cruel.

Not long after, Cardinal Beaton, of the old Scotch family of the Bethunes, who was Papal Legate and Primate of the Catholic Scotch Church, was assassinated in revenge for Wishart's death. The assassins and their sympathisers, who were a goodly number, took up arms, seized and shut themselves up in the Castle of St. Andrews. John Knox went with them. Knox's admirers make out that he had no hand in the murder of the Cardinal. But that is most unlikely. He was at least an instigator, and accessory after the fact. His presence with the rebels in the fortress clearly points to that. His well-known violent and fanatical temper would alone go to show it. The royal troops, of course, immediately invested the place, but to prevent its destruction and further bloodshed, the garrison was permitted to surrender, and given a promise of their lives.

Knox was made to expiate his share by transportation to the galleys on the Loire, in France—

a dreadful sentence enough. The existence of
a galley slave then would make our penal ser-
vitude appear a luxury. Ever after he had a
horror of France and everything French, of which
his health, shattered by the rigorous winter he
spent in this awful punishment, was a lifelong
reminder. This explains his fierce and relentless opposition to the Scotch royal family, so
intimately allied, by marriage, to the French
Court.

After nine months his amnesty was procured by
influence from England, but he deemed it unsafe to
return to Scotland. It was then he wandered over
to Geneva to visit Calvin. He had heard of him
before. Wishart had seen him too, and in their
frequent talks he must have been often mentioned.
Through Calvin's influence Knox got charge of a
Swiss congregration. But he did not hold the
incumbency very long. There was a wider field for
mischief, or, as he thought, reform, awaiting him
in Scotland, and he tried to get there. He went
homeward by way of England, and not finding things
quite safe yet for his return, he stayed there. He
secured a living as a priest again from the Bishop
of Durham. For though England was in schism, it
was not yet in heresy, and all the old Catholic rites
and practices still prevailed. Here he improved
his " shining hours " by paying court to a former

acquaintance, one Margery Bowes, and married her.
This and other things were too much for his Lord-
ship of Durham, and he was cashiered. Meanwhile, revolutionary politics were in the ascendant
in Scotland, and soon the way for Knox's entrance
was clear, and his return was celebrated by quite
an ovation from his numerous friends and sup-
porters. Then commenced that triumphant and
destructive progress through his native land, during
which every vestige of the old faith was over-
thrown. Smoking ruins of abbeys, monasteries, and
convents marked his path. The inmates, of both
sexes, were ruthlessly slain when they did not make
good their flight into a penniless exile. The
opposition and hatred aroused against the Catholic
reigning family, on account of its French blood,
gave a patriotic colour to these deeds of rapine,
and facilitated and hastened the consummation.
Thus the new religion of Scotland, planted in
slaughter and watered in blood, was introduced and
established. Knox was, all through the business,
the same two-handed swordsman who marched before
Wishart in the years gone by—grim, stern, merciless,
uncompromising. Such was the man who gave the
Scotch, except the poor, faithful Highlanders, their
new religion. Now, how do you like him? I
do not think you will find in veracious history
anything to modify that sketch. You will find a

deal of declamation in his panegyrists, but strip
off the rhetoric, and only that remains. It may
enhance your opinion, or otherwise, to learn that
this too uxorious old priest had the effrontery, in
his sixtieth year, to lead a mere child—a girl of
fifteen years—to the altar, as if in mockery of the
vow there sealed between his soul and God so long
before, to serve Him in celibacy.

The version of Christian faith that he imported
from Geneva, though freed from many of the curbs
to human frailty imposed by the Catholic Church,
was, like its founder in Scotland, of a grim and
uninviting kind—a joyless Sabbatarianism, and that
most terrible of libels on God's mercy and justice
—predestinarianism. As a natural consequence a
reaction against it *among the educated* has gradually
taken place, under the lead of men like Reid and
Hume, while Carlyle dealt it a death-blow. But
unfortunately under such leading the reaction has
not been in favour of the old faith or any faith.
It has been in the direction of a far more dismal
Agnosticism, where men are afloat on the sea of life
without a chart to guide, or compass to steer by, or
helm to direct, and not one small beacon-light of hope
touching their darkness from the eternal shore.
There is no one man more accountable for this
hopeless state of soul among his educated fellow-
countrymen—and nowadays most Scotchmen are

educated—than Thomas Carlyle. They are almost
idolatrously proud of him; and as far as rare
literary excellence, scholarship, and bold original
genius go, that pride in him is more or less justifi-
able. His influence on them consequently has been
enormous. But, oh! it is malign influence. Every
volume of this man smacks of the infallible seer, of
almost a self-constituted god, and from every page
breathes a quintessence of human pride. He seems
consumed by more than the *sæva indignatio* of Swift.
He is the grand indictment-drawer against the
Omnipotent Disposer of all things sublunar. He
really wants you to believe that if he, Thomas Carlyle, had been at the Creator's side he would have
saved Him many a blunder, and it was a great mistake that he was not there to improve Him by
his infallible judgment about all things. But that
mistake having, for the misfortune of the world, irre-
trievably happened, he leaves you under no erroneous
impression that, even at this eleventh hour, there
can be any appeal from that Carlylean judgment.
The chronic dyspepsia of body which so pitifully
afflicted the poor man, seems to have attacked his
mind, for in no other author will you find so
sustained a growl and grumble, so snappish a sneer
and snarl—a kind of running accompaniment of
dominant but discordant notes to the harmony of
his omniscience. At times, as we wade through the

turbid and boulder-strewn stream of his eloquence,
we are reminded now of Diogenes, the growling
philosopher, and now of Thersites, son of Agrius,
Homer's ugly and dirty scold. Now all this, from
the immense power of the man, insensibly but
necessarily affects the minds of his readers. They,
too, become dissatisfied with the arrangement of
things — uselessly, most uselessly, because they
cannot re-arrange them in the least particular—
and from mistrusting God, they come to doubt
Him and to deny, or, at least, ignore Him. Now,
if Mr. Carlyle and his forebears in Scotch scep-
ticism could do something really practical, such as
abolish death, decree that pain shall no longer be
the heirloom of human life, or even give us un-
decayable teeth, they might have some claims to
our respect. But you know perfectly well they
cannot do any of these things. The most he,
Carlyle, and a fellow-Agnostic, Tyndall, did for
the human race in this line, by united effort, was
to stop in a walk and a talk they were having
together one day, and shake hands with each other,
for having "abolished hell." But would it not be
as great an act of faith to believe these gentlemen
on this point as to believe the Bible ?

But the Scotch are too shrewd and clever to
remain satisfied long with the empty egg-shell of
Agnosticism. My belief is that the Scotch will

come back again to the sure hope of the old faith, and I have a private opinion that they will be an influential element in bringing England back too. They are to-day the brain-carriers of the British race. They have been the builders and the pillars of England's Colonial Empire. They are next to the Jews in commercial ability, and far surpass them in honesty and integrity. There is some foundation, then, for the opinion that if the Scotch come back they will turn too the religious tide of England, if it ever is to be turned, into the old channel from which their sixteenth-century fore-fathers diverted it. But pity of pities will it be, if, in disappointment of this hope, this fine race, this *fine fleur* of trained human intelligence, will elect to go down with the universal wreck in that paganism to which educated Protestantism is inevitably hastening.

IV.—ENGLAND'S CASE.

WHILE the religious disturbance in Germany was going on, the Catholic Church in England, at the opening of Henry VIII.'s reign, was never more flourishing or had brighter prospects. There were two Universities, which, on the testimony of Erasmus, were centres of creditable learning and homes of righteous living. Splendid abbeys and

G

monasteries were numerous through the land, where
the poor always had their portion, instruction, and
spiritual service. Those grand minsters, built by
the monks of long ago, which even modern genius
has been unable to rival in sublimity of design,
were already centuries old, and served by the
Grey Friars and Black Friars and White Friars,
and Crutched (a corruption of *Crossed*) Friars, as
the people loved familiarly to call the members
of the old religious Orders. There was a perfect
hierarchy, headed by the Primate of Canterbury, in
intimate union with Rome. There was a Cardinal
Legate of the Pope resident at the court. There
was a young king of much talent and great promise.
He was an earnest and zealous Catholic, so much
so that when Luther's reforming manœuvres became
known to him he was indignant. He was so zealous
for the faith that, with an industry not often found
in princes, he took up his pen and composed a long
theological treatise in refutation of him. He sent
a copy to the Pope, who, in grateful recognition,
conferred on him the title of "Defensor Fidei,"
which you still may see on the coins of the realm.
When the news of Luther's sacrilegious marriage
arrived, he was so moved that he wrote him a personal reprimand in no measured terms, and besought
him to hide his shame from the public view, as a
monk and nun in wedlock were a scandal to all

Europe. From the safe distance of Saxony, Luther sent a characteristic answer. The virulence and insolence of his language were beyond all bounds. He called the king "a crowned ass," "a varlet," "a liar," "a swine of the scholastic herd." "Henry," he said, "thou art a fool." Is was well for the ex-friar that he was out of that fool's reach. As it was, Henry tried by political influence to have him seized and punished, and he came near putting an end to Luther and Lutheranism.

So serene was the sky above England's Catho-licism at this time that no one foresaw the coming storm which was to wreck the faith of a thousand years. What was it destroyed so fair a peace? Alas for human virtue exposed to temptation! It was a genuine case of *cherchez la femme*. She has been in all our troubles since the greatest of them all at the beginning. Yet, in many instances, as, I think, in this case, more "sinned against than sinning." Henry had early married a Spanish princess of piety, culture, and amiable disposition, and with her had passed eighteen years of wedded content. Katherine was plain-looking and getting old, and the king looked on a handsome maid of honour in the way forbidden by our Lord—"so as to desire her in his heart." The ease and leisure, the luxurious surroundings that great wealth sup-plies in court life, make it, as all history witnesses,

the very nursery of temptation, the forcing-house of
carnal sin. Henry did not escape. But no man becomes suddenly bad. Nor did he. He had scruples,
and sincerely wished to avoid scandal. So with
great cleverness he made out an ingenious case for
divorce. He was too instructed not to know that the
Church never grants a divorce between people once
validly married. She declares it, has always declared, and will always declare it beyond her powers.
Valid marriage, once consummated, is indissoluble
by divine decree, for the peace and preservation of
Christian society, and with that decree neither she
nor any earthly power is competent to interfere.
Henry never asked for a divorce in this sense. He
alleged that he never had been validly married, and
submitted his case to the Holy See to decide whether
that was so or not on the reasons he put forth. If
it turned out that he really never had been married,
why then by the very fact he could marry Anne
Boleyn lawfully and validly. The reasons he gave
were—that he had espoused his brother's widow;
that though a dispensation had been granted in due
form for his marriage he now doubted whether such
dispensation *could* have been granted, as the case is
expressly forbidden in the Old Testament; and that
even if it could the causes given in the petition
were not sufficient or did not exist at all, such as
that one about preventing a war between Spain and

England. History has long ago decided that this
is what is known in common phrase as a bogus
case, and we need not enter into its tedious, lengthy,
and miserable story. With wonderful tenacity and
a really exemplary patience Henry argued it and
pursued it for two years. Some censure has been
passed on Pope Clement for opening such a suspicious and flimsy case at all, and upsetting the kingdom by sending a special envoy and erecting a
tribunal extraordinary in England, the King and
Queen being summoned to give evidence against
each other. It would have been more honest to
say from the start, "the thing cannot be done—
it is rather late in the day, after eighteen years
with the rights of a royal lady and the legitimacy
of her offspring at stake, for us to believe in or
entertain your scruples—it cannot be granted." To
assert this is most unfair. Henry had always been a
loyal and faithful son of the Church. He was on the
most friendly and intimate terms with the Pope. He
was the distinguished monarch of a great Catholic
nation. He therefore deserved every deference and
respect. It would have been unseemly, it would
have been stupid, to treat him as an ordinary
private individual. There was nothing that the
Pope could lawfully do for him, no trouble that he
could take to oblige him in any way, that would
not have been only common wisdom, and he, the

king, was fully entitled to expect it. So, great
pains and patience were shown on both sides, and
everything that could possibly be done to decide
the matter fairly and peacefully was attempted.
The king many a time grew restive and impatient,
but though urged by less scrupulous courtiers to
act in the German fashion then prevailing, notably
by Cromwell—not Oliver, but Thomas—celebrated
in Shakspeare's play on the subject (which, by the
way, is very vile history), yet he always recoiled
from the grave step of re-marrying without the
sanction of the Head of the Church.   This was an
indication that all might yet be well, and that he
would listen to the Pope's voice with submission
when he decided, had there not come just then a
cry of distress—an appeal from the object or the
victim of his passion, to save her honour.   The
child she was thus unlawfully bearing was the
future queen—Elizabeth.

   This precipitated matters, and without further to
do a secret marriage was performed in the Royal
Chapel by a complaisant courtier-priest named Lee.
Some say that it was a Father George Brown,
Prior of the Austin Friars, afterwards made Archbishop of Dublin in reward for this.   Wearied with
the prolonged negotiations, and bewildered by the
judicial proceedings, conducted in a tongue she
only half understood, Katherine had placed her

case in the hands of the Pope by appeal. When her advocate had related her side of the story, and had now to add news of the secret marriage, Clement VII. determined, like Pope Nicholas in the case of the Empress Theodora, to shield with his great authority this wronged and heart-broken lady—a foreigner in a strange country—so cruelly treated by him who was plighted to cherish her. And as the Greeks were allowed to go out from the Church's unity, so should England and England's king, rather than that injustice should be condoned. He commanded Henry to restore to all her rights his lawful wife Katherine and put Anne Boleyn away, and if he did not comply he should be excommunicated from the Church. Now came the rupture. The king rose in all his pride and anger against this action of the Pope. He openly and violently renounced all allegiance to the Holy See, and proclaimed what was henceforth to be known as the Royal Supremacy over the Church of England. Thus was a nation's faith, the sacred tradition of nine centuries of Catholic life, and the hallowed memories that hung about altar, shrine, and cloister, blighted and bartered for the lust of a despot.

King Henry was once good—as good and as able a man as ever sat on England's throne. He did not become bad all at once, but when he did become so, it was the *corruptio optimi pessima.*

Impartial history has from that moment written
him down, and *pace* Mr. Froude, will continue to
write him down—a monster. He married in all,
before he had done, six women. The heads of
two of them he cut off, and two of them he
divorced. Any one who dared to censure his conduct, and who even abstained from approving it,
or refused to acknowledge his spiritual supremacy,
he mercilessly sacrificed, no matter how close the
former friendship. He raged furiously. In fact,
for the rest of his reign his conduct was mere
animal fury. He drenched England in its best
blood. The gentle and saintly Bishop of Roch-
ester—Fisher, the tutor of his boyhood, and whom
he long loved beyond all other men, was thrown
into the Tower and died at the block. The learned
and accomplished chancellor, Sir Thomas More, a
man of stainless and blameless career, shared the
same opprobrious fate. The great statesman
Wolsey, who had made England a nation to be
reckoned with in the councils of Europe, and
given her rank as a first-class power, for hesitating
between this transformed king and the deep sea
of Papal censure, had to bid "farewell—a long
farewell to all his greatness," and only the timely
mercy of a broken heart cut short his days, he
too would have ended on the scaffold. Henry
was once a great friend and admirer of the friar

priests. Mr. Mivart, in one of the interesting papers of his Miscellanies, quotes a letter from the king to the Pope, in which he eulogises the good fathers of the Abbey at Greenwich, close by his summer palace, and speaks of them as blessings to his kingdom. The essayist then proceeds to tell eloquently the terrible fate to which Henry afterwards subjected these same men, and the horrible and hateful cruelties practised on 200 of their brethren at his bidding, because they would not take him for their Pope. The non-jurors, who were chiefly of the religious Orders and the owners of the rich Abbeys, were all dispossessed and driven away or suffered death in various cruel ways, while the royal coffers were replenished with the patrimonies of the poor, and the royal favourites got grants of those rich lands which their descendants still hold. To Anne Boleyn he made a present of the smilingest garden of them all, Fountains Abbey in Yorkshire, not long before he beheaded the poor creature. It was thus the shadow of a great sorrow spread over happy England, conjured by the hand of a single man in those wretched days of irresponsible, despotic, one-man power!

There is one incident of this juncture too significant to pass over. The news of Henry's outbreak against the Pope was welcome grist to

Luther's mill, and, forgetful of their former not
too amiable correspondence, he hastened to greet
him in a letter full of warm praise and grovelling
fulsome flattery.   Henry treated him with scorn-
ful silence.   He might be angry with the Pope,
but he never could bear Luther, and kept Lutheranism far from England while he lived.   He
plunged England in schism, but he drew the line
at heresy—the change of doctrine.   In that respect he remained as orthodox as any Pope.   He
even left £500 to found a daily requiem Mass
for his soul.   I wonder what has become of that
money.

Being so orthodox, he, of course, must have
his Primate and his hierarchy.   He was not very
blessed in his choice.   Indeed, he had not much
to choose from.   He killed all the good men.
The English Cardinal, Pole, who was his own
blood-relation and whom at one time he prized
very highly, he forbade the kingdom under pain
of death, because he had the audacity to reprimand him and dissuade him from his obstinate
courses.   Cardinal Pole had to find employment
abroad.

The man who first filled the See of Canterbury
and conformed in everything to the king's behests
was a kind of small Photius in intrigue and un-
scrupulousness.   When the divorce question was

pending, he observed that all who sided with or aided the king in any way found the surest way to royal favour. So he determined to contribute some striking and novel argument to the controversy. Though then only in an obscure living in Devonshire, he found a friend at court, and commissioned him to watch an opportunity of imparting his idea to his Majesty. This courtier one day, in the hearing of the king, mentioned in quite a casual way, that Dr. Cranmer's plan of taking a consensus of opinion for the divorce case from all the Universities of Europe seemed a capital idea. The bait took immediately. The king said, "Yes, yes, the very thing; I like that. Who is this Dr. Cranmer? I must see him. Marry, I trow he has got the right sow by the ear." So to the king Cranmer was brought. His fortune was made from that day—or his misfortune, if you view it in another light.

The man's antecedents were not very reputable. Admitted on a poor scholarship to the schools of Cambridge, he got involved in a low love affair with a barmaid of the town, nicknamed Black Joan. He was compelled to marry her and quit the University. On her death in childbed, he managed somehow to get back, and pursued his studies until he was ordained. He left no name for talent or much learning in Cambridge. He

filled several minor benefices until he brought
himself under the king's notice as above described.
The first mark of the royal patronage was his
promotion to the Archdeaconry of Taunton.   Soon
after, with a well-filled purse and royal letters,
he was despatched into Germany to carry out his
own suggestion.   Here he encountered many of
the leading Lutherans.   He admired their methods
so much that the memory of his old game at Cambridge came back strongly upon him, and to while
away his leisure he paid court, this venerable archdeacon, to a girl of the house he was staying in
—a niece of the very Osiander whom Luther sent
into Brandenburg to pervert the Teutonic Knights—
and finally married her.   During his absence the see
of Canterbury became vacant, whereupon Henry,
knowing he would find only a too complacent
instrument of his desires in his new friend, nomi-
nated him for this great place.   The Pope, who
was ignorant of the man's bad character, as a
mark of favour to the king, who was not yet excommunicated, immediately confirmed the appointment, so that while the Primatial pallium was
going from Rome into England by one way, Dr.
Cranmer was journeying homeward with his
German Frau by another.   Not sure of Henry's
temper, he dared not acknowledge her, so he established her secretly in London while he hied him

to his consecration in the splendid minster by
the Thames. This was the first time that so
scandalous a piece of impiety was enacted in England—that a secret wife should sit peering from
behind a pillar, and probably laughing in her muff
at the archiepiscopal consecration of her husband.
It is more than likely that Henry got some side-
wind of this. If so, he played a very grim jest
on his new Primate, and at the same time conveyed
a very telling hint. A royal decree was sent to
him, in which the king set forth that certain
priests having attempted secret and illegal mar-
riages, the penalty for this offence was death, and
he charged the Primate to report on such cases.
The white terror that seized his Grace may be
imagined. He hurried to the lodgings in Lambeth.
" Meine Frau," he said, " look at this—you would
not have your loving husband killed, would you?
You must go back for a while to uncle Osiander."
So he packed her up in a perforated box, and had
her smuggled out of the country, labelled most
probably—*German merchandise returned ; ordered
too soon.* Then he turned his attention to the
married clergy, and charged those clerical ruffians
to observe their sacred vows! He shared, of
course, in Henry's excommunication when it came.
What mattered the Pope to him while his royal
master was his friend! So with a light heart he

became the first schismatical Archbishop of Canterbury. Everything went on as in Catholic times. The king wished it so. And when Henry died, Cranmer buried him with a solemn Requiem Mass, of which he was the celebrant. When we think of what he said and did a little later against this rite, so dear and sacred to Catholics, we are amazed at the reckless hypocrisy of this man.

Edward was a boy of ten when he succeeded his father. This threw the supreme authority in Church affairs into the hands of Cranmer. He then revealed himself in his true colours. He began to stamp out the Catholic religion in England. Henry had retained all its rites and doctrines. He abolished both. He fetched his wife back from Germany, as the most effective way of ending clerical celibacy. He took away the altars, and broke up the tabernacles. Neither Mass nor Real Presence were to be any longer in the creed of England. He published forty-one articles, afterwards reduced to the famous thirty-nine, embodying the new creed—all out of his own head—and backed them up by the most drastic anti-Catholic laws—the cruel statutes of Edward VI. One of the most fearful persecutions that ever disgraced any country followed the application of these laws. Edward was a boy-king, but by no means a cipher. Under Cranmer's tutelage he soon learned

to delight in signing death-warrants, even for
persons nearly related to him. Horrible spectacle
to see this terrible child dabbling his young hands
smilingly in kindred's blood—truly a worthy son
of a tyrant sire. His reign was a short one. The
next in legal succession was his half-sister, another
of Henry's children, Mary Tudor. This is the lady
who is known in some non-Catholic histories by
the coarse and vulgar epithet of "Bloody" Mary.
There is something most unmanly and unfair in
this. There is no doubt that as Mary was stanch
and convinced in her Catholic ways, she deemed
herself bound to undo what must have appeared
in her eyes the great wrong done by Cranmer and
his followers to her faith; and though for the first
three of the five years of her reign she moved
cautiously and tolerantly enough, for some reasons
. things then got more or less out of her hands, and
her advisers and agents savagely retaliated for the
confiscations and tortures and burnings perpetrated
under Edward by similar burnings and tortures
and confiscations. But why give the exclusive op-
probrium of "bloody" to her name? Why not
"bloody" King Henry and "bloody" King Edward,
and "bloody" Queen Elizabeth, the bloodiest of them
all? If, in Mary's reign a rivulet of blood was shed,
they spilt rivers of it. For which "a plague on all
their houses," if you like; but let us be fair.

Besides, the slight extenuation of the reasons above alluded to must be pleaded for Mary. The sequel of her unfortunate marriage with Philip of Spain left her a broken-hearted woman. Broken health, added to a broken heart, deadened all her interest in public affairs, and an early death fortunately ended a great unhappiness.

Retribution came for Cranmer as well as others in these terrible days. He suffered one of those dreadful ends by fire, which, in our times of humaner feeling, we all so very much deplore.

A knowledge of Cranmer's character ought to set at rest for ever all question of Anglican Orders. How could he, who had no reverence for anything sacred, be supposed to perform seriously any sacred action? Besides, he had no *intention* of doing what the Church does in conferring Orders. Neither had his creature-bishops. Now the defect of due intention in the minister invalidates a sacrament. Therefore, all attempts to confer Orders in the Anglican establishment are vitiated *in radice* by defect of this intention. Holy Orders do not there exist, nor, as a consequence, can any real priesthood there be found. Let not our separated brethren blame us for the statement. It is only the rigid consequence of an irreversible historical fact.[1]

---

[1] The recently-published Bull on Anglican Orders bears out what was here said a year before.

V.—ELIZABETH

WHATEVER hope there was of restoring England to Catholic Unity under Mary Tudor was dispelled soon after the accession of Elizabeth. Both had inherited a good deal of mental ability and strength of purpose from their father, Henry VIII. But while Mary had from her Spanish mother a strong sense of faith and personal piety, Elizabeth had some very opposite qualities from Anne Boleyn. Vanity was with her not the ordinary female foible; it was a passion. A love of lavish display and worldliness characterised her whole career. Extreme frivolity and freedom from restraint were noticeable from her early years. In the lifetime of her father, when she was only sixteen, her relations with Seymour the Admiral, one of her father's numerous brothers-in-law, were made the subject of public inquiry. All through her life she was ever playing with the absorbing and dangerous excitement of love affairs. When she was queen she was as capricious about her male favourites as her father was in the matter of wives, and beheaded quite as many of them.

It will at once be seen that the Catholic faith, which exacts a far higher and purer conduct than that, and imposes so many wholesome, if irksome,

H

restraints, had small chance of favour from a loose
liver like Elizabeth. For her anti-Catholic feeling,
as exhibited by her complicity in the rebellion of
that dissolute and reckless knight, Thomas Wyatt,
Mary, for a time, confined her to the Tower. Yet,
strange to say, on her own accession she seemed
to contemplate, for a brief moment, continuing the
work of re-establishing the old faith. The sign of
this was the sending of an embassy to Rome to
announce her accession to the throne, and pray for
the Pope's recognition. It is idle now to speculate
whether this was a sincere move on her part towards
union with the Church, or whether it was done from
policy to forestall trouble from Philip II., who on
hearing of his wife's demise was already advancing
his claim to sovereignty in England. Anyhow, the
Pope refused to recognise her. His predecessor
had excommunicated her father for a bigamous marriage with her mother. That marriage had been
declared null and void, and in the eyes of the
Church she was illegitimate, and even by the laws
of England ineligible to the throne. How could
he then, with any consistency or sense of justice,
accede to her prayer, no matter how strongly he may
have felt impelled, on the other hand, to avail himself
of so fair an opportunity for securing the re-estab-
lishment of Catholicity ? Even all England Catholic
again could not be price enough for unworthy and

time-serving flattery, and saying yes to what he must have believed to be a lie. Yet some non-Catholic writers, swayed by their prevalent prejudice which keeps them from rising to the level of any nobleness of sentiment in an opponent, only see in this but a piece of Papal insolence.

To a woman of Elizabeth's haughty and imperious temper, the Pope's reply was the never-to-be-forgiven slight, and she proceeded to take her revenge. She hurled back defiance, and vowed the utter abolition of all things Catholic. She evoked the ghost of Cranmer. His Thirty - nine Articles and Common Prayer Book ritual were introduced again. The old weary, shameful work of plunder, prison, and stake began once more. The pitiless hand of iron and heart of adamant she used, in this and all her works, was Robert, Lord Cecil, the progenitor of England's present Premier, Lord Salisbury. The complete discomfiture of Philip in his expedition to recover his rights in the British throne—the wreck of his " Invincible Armada," when the very winds in their courses fought for Elizabeth, left her free scope for her vengeance. Not all the years of the longest reign among England's queens were enough to satiate it, and when that reign ended, almost the only trace of the Catholic faith, whose special home England had been for nine hundred years, was the ruins of its splendid abbey churches scattered up and down the land.

I once stood within the crumbling walls of the grandest of them, amid the smiling hills of York-shire, and I thought how mysterious it was that this and hundreds like it, throughout the length and breadth of the country, should still be there. Are they not like accusing spirits—disinherited ghosts of an unforgotten past, wrapt in the mourn-ing vesture of their drooping ivy, lifting up their mutilated arms, and dumbly pleading to living ears to give them back the glory and the beauty and the divine joy of the service that once was theirs? Will that mute and touching pleading go for ever unheard?

.   .   .   .   .

Before leaving this historical phase of the question, in which I have endeavoured to set out, as plainly and as truthfully as I could, the causes of religious disunion in Christendom, there are two things incidental to them which it will be necessary to touch on. They are points that generally prove a stumbling-block to our separated brethren, and often not unembarrassing to ourselves.

The first is the coercive power employed in the past to preserve the unity of faith.

The second is the undeniable temporal prosperity that has marked the career of the separated nations.

1. Of course it seems very horrible to many to read that men were imprisoned and tortured, and burned at the stake, for taking the liberty of openly denying and rejecting certain tenets of the Christian faith. But this is a mere question of degree, of the usages of other times, and of sentiment. Let us get at the principle — the fundamental reason—why men were punished for this thing, and we shall then perhaps be able to think more calmly on the matter. We find this principle in the words used by the Founder of Christianity, to those whom He commissioned to teach it: "Go ye into the whole world and preach this gospel to every creature — he that believeth and is baptized *shall be saved*, but he that believeth not *shall be condemned*" (Mark, 16th chapter). Now this is a very grave and very awful sanction attached to this *belief*, which they were charged to impose on every creature. It involves not a question of mere temporal life and death, but of eternal life and eternal death. If these men and their successors really believed this, how could they stand by in indifference, while any one who chose was playing havoc with that belief—denying it—upsetting it—changing it—paring it down and whittling it away? They would be no men if they did. Their sense of honour, of faithfulness, of responsibility, should at once move them to use

every means in their power to stop what they were
bound to think was such dire and destructive mischief.   What is usually said of the trusted employee
who looks on at the plundering and destruction of
his master's property ?   Why, that he is a scoundrel
and a villain.   And would the others be anything
less ?   Was there ever a State Government that
had a contented tolerance for any one who violently
assailed the institutions of the country, or despised
its laws ?   Let the prisons, and the chain-gangs,
and the gibbets, to be found wherever you travel,
be the answer.   And is the divinely-founded spiritual
society less than the human and the temporal ?   Is
it to get no protection from conspirators and law-
breakers ?   The rulers of nations before the sixteenth
century, who were honest in their profession of
Christianity, did not think so.   As early as the
middle of the fourth century the Emperor Theo-
dosius enacted severe civil penalties against any one
disturbing the religious peace, or advancing his own
private opinion against the recognised teaching and
governing authority of the Church.   So did Hono-
rius, and Justinian, and Charlemagne, and Frederick
II. of Germany, and Charles V.   The last-named,
as head of the Empire, combated German Protestantism for twenty years, and at length took up
arms against the Protestant princes after the Diets
of Spires and Augsburg and the League of Smal-

kald, where they rejected his advice and his authority. He inflicted a crushing defeat upon them,
and would have ended this Protestant schism, but
for the treachery of his chief-of-staff, and once
trusted friend, Maurice of Saxony.

Were the Popes, when they had the power, expected to be the less zealous for the unity and
truth than they? The means they used for securing
them were, first, assembling General Councils in times
of dispute and denial, and solemnly proposing what
the prelates from various regions agreed upon as
the traditional and true doctrines of Christianity;
and, secondly, by inviting the co-operation of all
Christian rulers and governments, to see that these
decisions, which were not mere figments of human
minds, but were revealed commands and messages
of God to His creatures, were respected. Surely,
seeing that they believed themselves commissioned
by Him to preserve and hand on this revelation
so vitally bound up with men's eternal welfare,
who can say that this was anything but their
obvious duty? But then, what about this dreadful Inquisition, with its racks, and screws, and
burnings? Yes, this institution has got such a
bad name any time these three hundred years that
people shudder at it now. Still the word itself is
a very harmless one—it means inquiry. The tribunal was a court of reference for the temporal

rulers to determine who was and who was not
tampering with and undermining the received religion of the State. It deliberated on heresy and
heretics. These have also come to be offensive
labels. Heresy is a Greek word, which means a
choosing, and a heretic is a man who chooses. In
religion you see at once how wrong and how proud
it is for any one to arrogate a private and individual choice in the matter for himself, since it is
fixed for all time by divine authority. At one
time Christian rulers and States saw this, and consented to restrain and punish the wrong-doers.
To determine who they were they deferred to the
courts of inquiry, whose office it was to examine
the novel doctrines propounded by these free-choice
advocates—that was the Inquisition. Its functions
ceased with the inquiry, and handing over the
heretic with their decision to the "secular arm."
And all these pictures, that appeal so strongly to
prejudice and passion, of men in religious garb
applying instruments of torture to expiring wretches,
or carrying burning brands to ignite the fatal
fagots, are nothing but painted lies. The inquisi-
tors were men of religious orders, whose mission was
mercy, not fiendish cruelty. They always sought
the conversion of the mistaken wrong-doers before
delivering them to the civil power. But they
remaining obstinate, it was no part of mercy to say,

"Let these men go free again to destroy the faith and imperil the eternal safety of hundreds and thousands of other souls." Better one should perish legally than that so many should, in their conviction, perish eternally. And if the penalties meted out by the secular authorities of those days were, in our more humane views, horrible and barbarous, we may deplore them, and be glad they are gone; but we must remember they were the universal usage, and applied not to heretics alone, but to all manner of malefactors. Modes of execution and torturing punishments change, but they go on all the same. They are going on yet everywhere—except that crimes against God and His faith and holy religion are those only which in our enlightened times are exempted from them. Those easy-minded and softly-speaking people who say, "Oh, it is so much nicer not to bother people about religion; every one should be allowed to be perfectly free to believe exactly what he likes, and say out what he thinks—what does it matter?" are either strangely ignorant or culpably thoughtless of those dread words of our Lord, "And he who believeth not (*what I have commanded you to teach*) shall be condemned."

2. There is no doubt that, as far as worldly greatness and prosperity go, the countries that have separated from Catholic unity look as if they had

been greatly blessed for doing so, while the reverse is the case of the nations that remained.

It is true that Russia has grown in such proportions and strength that people now call her the Colossus of the North.

The German arms have now been carried in victory over a third of Europe. In bewildering defeat the two great Catholic powers, Austria and France, have gone down before them, and the German Empire occupies to-day the most commanding political eminence in the world.

The case of England is still more wonderful. Her achievements for the last few centuries stand first in all history. A little country out on the north-west fringe of Europe, she has got possession of and is able to hold immense and populous regions in the Indies, ten thousand miles from her shores. Hindoos and Moslems, Burmans and Malays, she rules by the hundred million. With the Roman orator she might ask, "*Quæ regio in terris nostri non plena laboris?*" And if she has lost the best part of North America as a dependency, it may still be her boast that there are over sixty millions there to-day speaking the English tongue, thus proclaiming, and to proclaim for all time, the origin of this now truly astonishing country and mightiest of Republics. Then think of her vast wealth and world-wide commerce. It used to be said that its sails whitened the seas; now the metaphor is more grimy, but just as expressive—its smoke blackens the skies. In face of all this, the non-Catholic shakes hands with himself, so to say, and thinks he is specially favoured by Heaven for having saved the world from the errors of Popery—this is no fancy, it is a boast of theirs; while the Catholic, if he is the least bit worldly - minded, feels a troubling uneasiness about it, and is tempted to say that God has been kinder to his enemies than to him.

This would be quite true if the Divine Founder of the Church had promised temporal prosperity to His followers as a reward for their fidelity. But everybody knows He did nothing of the kind. It was all the other way. "Blessed are ye when men shall curse ye, and persecute ye, and say every evil against ye, lying, on account of Me, and when men shall hate ye, and cut ye off, and revile ye, and cast out your name as an evil thing on account of the Son of Man—be ye glad and rejoice, for your reward is very great in heaven."

The "hundred-fold" only applies to the followers of the counsels of perfection, and those sublime and superhuman renunciations are not to be found in the story of conquering nations.

There is, beside, a very disquieting sentence in Ecclesiasticus, chap. v.: "Do not say—well, I have sinned, and nothing unprosperous has happened to me, for a patient avenger is the Most High God."

It is also to be remembered that there have been nations very wicked and idolatrous as great and as prosperous in their days as the above-named are in ours. So you see that is not a too reliable sign of Heaven's special regard. Rather have the old nations become striking examples of the action of the "patient Avenger."

Moreover, men's natural gifts are the active secondary providence in the world. By the ingenious and free use of them men may carry themselves to any height of greatness or wickedness that they please for *their* time, without that God ever visibly or miraculously interferes, until *His* time of reckoning comes—as it surely will. To that dread time in all things religious—moral and doctrinal—lies the ultimate appeal.

Finally, the outward renown of nations is no standard for the real happiness of the people they include. I have been in the back settlements of America, the back "blocks" of the Southern Hemisphere, and through some English shires. I have seen there as dreary and dismal and cheerless misery and unhappiness as one could well find in this tearful vale, while up and down through Ireland I have found a people proverbially poor, hated and despised, cruelly wronged, and until lately, in legal serfdom

on the land they lived by,. yet cheery and light-
hearted and happy—far more so than the crowds
in other lands overshadowed by the glamour of
national greatness. Most of them think they would
be happier with Home Rule or as an independent
nation. If they remain as profoundly attached to
their faith, as, in the main, they are now, they may
be—for that is an indispensable condition of their
happiness.

PART IV

THE CHURCH'S ANSWER TO THE REFORMERS

I.—True Reform

From all the foregoing pitiful story of the causes of Disunion which candour obliged us to tell, some may fancy that the Catholic Church was reduced to the lethargic state of the dying in the sixteenth century. It was far from that. A divine word was pledged against her failing. In the time when that awful storm was passing, and when things must have looked ruinously dark, there were many, many souls left who were stayed and strengthened by that promise, " Behold, I am with you all days, even to the end of the world." And the memory of that other and prophetic storm of Genesareth was with them too. Christ was asleep in the boat of His disciples. The driving wind and threatening waves made them think their end had come. They called Him with a frightened cry, " Master, save us, we are perishing." " Why are ye afraid, O ye men of little faith ? " He said, and rising up He commanded the wind and the waves, and there came a great calm, and presently the boat was at the shore. The same Divine Master whom the wind and the waves obeyed, is still here to calm the storm that the passions of men can raise around the bark of His Church. So they believed, and their trust did not mislead. Peter's successor was there too in the Roman See; and to that head and centre of authority all who loved peace and looked for guidance turned in this sixteenth century. And first of all to turn to it was the Catholic Emperor, Charles V. There was no greater monarch since Charlemagne, perhaps, and in our century the only one who rivals him at all, as a ruler and a general, is the first Napoleon. It was his desire and his task for twenty years to reconcile Germany to the Church. He had many meetings and consultations with Clement VII. and Paul III., the Pontiffs reigning in his time, and constantly urged the assembly of a general Council. But the times were too disturbed and too unhappy for that. The two leading Catholic sovereigns, he (Charles) and Francis I. of France, were, to the scandal of the faithful, almost constantly at war. Then the Turks were menacing and marauding all along the coast of Europe, and had to be repelled. It was no time to summon the representatives of the entire Church to assemble, nor could a Council be held in safety. But failing

the Council, the Emperor, on his part, attempted
all in his power by way of compromise with the
Protestants. He 'established what were known as
Colloquies. The most notable of them, and the last,
was held at Ratisbon. Melancthon, Bucer, and
others represented the *protesting* party, and the able
and learned Von Eck took up the Catholic cause.
To please the Emperor and show his goodwill at
any attempt at reconciliation, the Pope sent one of
the cardinals to preside as legate at this Colloquy.
But after lengthy discussion it was found that the
demands of the Protestants were far in excess of
the concessions which the Church was authorised
by her Divine Founder to make. They involved a
radical change in what He commanded her to
teach. So nothing came of these well-intentioned
negotiations.

Nor was the Pope inactive on his part. Legate
after legate was despatched into Germany, and if
their efforts were not everywhere successful, we
probably owe it to them that a third of that great
country still remains stanchly Catholic.

Pope Paul III., of the princely Farnesan family,
did a still more practical thing. He put a strong
and reforming hand to the abuses and indiscipline
in clerical life and Church régime, which gave real
grounds of complaint to the clamourers for reformation. He summoned to him three of the most

eminent and ablest of his cardinals, Caraffa (afterwards Pope), Sadoleti, and Conterini. " I am informed," he said, " of many things that need
correction in the administration of the Church.
While I take upon me to see nothing disedifying
shall continue in Rome and the Roman Curia, I
hereby appoint you a commission of inquiry for the
Church at large, and charge you to submit to me a
report of your labours."   They acted in this capacity
for a lengthened period.   They took evidence in
many places, found that there were many things to
be amended in respect to the collation of benefices,
the residence of those having cure of souls, the venal
seeking after office, dignities, and emoluments, the
presenting of untrained and uneducated youths for
orders, mendicancy and wandering about of monks,
and many other details of Church life calculated to
shake the confidence and shock the piety of the
laity.   The report submitted to the Pope was immediately acted upon in some particulars, and the
others he himself was able subsequently to submit
to the Council of Trent for legislation.   It may be
here remarked by any person of moderate observa-
tion, that if the discontents of Germany were moved
only with real zeal for the good of the Church, and
only honestly wished to have the blemishes incidental to the frailty of her human element removed,
they would have been satisfied with this without

I

going to the lengths of human pride in attacking
her teaching, sanctioned by the belief of fifteen
centuries, and throwing over the central authority
of the successors of St. Peter, to whom that authority
was committed by Christ Himself.   They knew full
well that there was nothing in that doctrine that
inculcated anything immoral or harmful to souls,
nothing in the definitions of Councils or instructions of Sovereign Pontiffs to countenance the
frailties that crept into the lives of those who served
in the sacred ministry and the spiritual institutions
of the Church.   Quite the contrary.   An impartial
inquirer would have seen in the public documents
of her history but the one desire to promote the
pure morality of the Christian life, to enjoin the
works that sanctified unto eternal salvation, and
to repeat to the world only the teachings of her
Divine Founder.   But these men were rebels, of bad
lives themselves, and led by recreant priests who
were false to their vows.   Oh, how uneasy ought the
followers of such people ever since to be !   It ought
not to be hard for them to see that if Christ had
any new ordinance to give, any vital change to re-
commend in His Church, *they* were not the men He
would be likely to choose.   In fact, it is but a mere
matter of plain history for them to find out that
they have been sadly misled, and are wandering
very far outside the pale of Christ's real Church.

II.—Some True Reformers

WHILE men of these times were noisily making such an ado about the revival of learning and letters, there were others just as busy, but in the quieter way of good and great souls, about the revival of piety and godly living. These were the true Reformers. One of them was Philip Neri, now known as one of the greatest of our modern saints, and even in his own days as the Apostle of Rome. Moved by the spectacle of extreme worldliness begotten by the new rage for pagan art and pagan letters, he began to remind people, in his gentle, winning way, that after all there were higher and better things to live for than that— things that made people really happy, because the thought of them kept them from sin, and nothing made real happiness so impossible as sin. That was all the burden of his simple message. But, oh! he made it so telling by the resistless example of his own life. Every stage of it was marked by a wonderful self-renouncement, a cheerful and generous giving himself away in the service of others, that they might be good, too, as he was, and as happy. If they were sinners, he offered to do their penances for them, though no one could say he ever sinned himself. If they were

in trouble, he prayed for them and took it away.
There, in Rome, he saw many things, no doubt,
that our Lord could not approve—much grandeur
and pomp among cardinals and prelates—but he
never said a grumbling word of them or against
them. He was charitable, and very humble and
unpresuming, and he went on his life of simple
holiness and preaching in his humble, cheery way,
and singing for gladness, and making others, even
the sad, sing too, and praying much and helping
others to pray and to hope, and never would
despair of anything or anybody, or hear of dis-
couragement, until his fame went out; and by-
and-by the great cardinals began to go to him,
and even Popes, to get his cheering word of
good counsel and his prayers, and even kiss his
hand, and he helped to make saints of some of
them, like Charles Borromeo and Pope Pius V.
Marvellous man and magnet of men and souls!
His was the charm and the spell of personal
holiness — of blameless and unselfish life. His
was not the noisy method of invective and de-
nunciation, and, like his divine model, he cried
not out in the streets. There was another priest
in the neighbouring city of Florence, Savonarola,
before alluded to, who tried the same thing and
failed—ruinously and disastrously failed. He was
a priest of the Order of Friar Preachers. He

was fiery and fierce, and lost respect for the office as well as the persons of those in high places—he lacked humility and its gentleness and persuasiveness—he forgot his vow of obedience and became a law to himself, and he who knows not how to obey never leads others well—he grew insubordinate and impatient of control, and finally fell foul of the most powerful family in Italy, the Medici. He was eventually convicted of heresy and schism, and executed in the public square of Florence. And what he tried to do, and could not do, for Florence, Philip did *exactly* for Rome and many another place, and was never molested—he was loved and venerated and canonised! because he went about it in the right way, as a really good, unselfish man should. The other was the fierce zealot, who could not forget himself, or, as Cardinal Newman so finely put it: " One was the wild voice of the whirlwind; the other was as the whisper of the fragrant air."

The only part, indeed, that Philip took in the fierce controversies of the time was a very small and simple one apparently, but fraught with a most important and lasting result. He said one day to a member of his community—for Philip gathered many able and pious men around him in his work, and enrolled them in an Order under the name of the Fathers of the Oratory: " They tell me, Father Baronius, that those poor heretics in Germany are publishing a history of the Church. They will be sure to write from their mistaken point of view, and in a light favourable to themselves and injurious to Holy Church. Well, I want you to write a history of the Church, too, in which you will vindicate the truth." Thus, in this light - hearted way, never doubting, did he impose a herculean labour on his friend. It cost him, before he had done with it, the patient labour of thirty years. But to that simple command, as simply obeyed, we owe the celebrated " Annals " of Cardinal Baronius, in which were laid the foundations of all scientific Church history.

Philip's mission, like all solid work, was not easy or rapid. It lasted all his own long lifetime. While he worked in Rome, his companions in his spirit extended their services through other cities of Italy, with a like happy result. Nor did this veritable reforming work end with him or them. The congregation he founded carries it on still. Not the least illustrious member of it was the late Cardinal Newman, and in Birmingham and Brompton to-day his spiritual children are doing what Philip began at Rome in the sixteenth century. As he forestalled and prevented the work of the Protestant Reformation in Italy, they are undoing it and repairing its mistakes in England, and have won back thousands of every rank and profession to the ancient faith of their fathers.

2. However, Philip was far from being the only one in these times who set his hand to this work of the revival of piety. There was Charles Borromeo, the great Archbishop of Milan, who, although a noble and a Cardinal (he became a Cardinal at the early age of twenty-nine), lived a life of austere and simple unselfish poverty nd sanctity. He was a bright example to his suffragan prelates and clergy, and a living sermon to his flock. He too founded a religious congregation of priests, called the Oblates. The Anglican Church gave to that Order one of its brightest ornaments in the person of the brilliant Archdeacon of Chichester, later known as Cardinal Manning. Any one acquainted with the daily life and untiring labour of the late Archbishop of Westminster, who knew also about St. Charles of Milan, could not but observe that he of the nineteenth century was the reproduction of him of the sixteenth.

3. There was also, at this time, St. Jerome Emilian. He was a member of a noble family in Venice, once an officer in the army and later on a priest. Like St. Philip and St. Charles, he enlisted others in the good works he undertook, and founded an Order. Besides missions throughout the north

of Italy, he established in various places, hospitals, orphanages, and refuges for the penitent.

4. There was St. Cajetan too, the founder of the Order known as the Theatines. They were named from the episcopal see of Theate, resigned by the first companion who joined. This was Peter Caraffa, before mentioned, who soon after became Pope. St. Cajetan did for Central and Southern Italy what Jerome Emilian did for the North. Von Ranke, the Protestant historian, pays a high tribute to him and the members of his Order. He confesses that to the active zeal and real piety of these men was due the re-action against Protestantism abroad in Europe towards the close of the sixteenth century, for their work extended into Germany, Poland, and Spain, besides Italy.

5. For similar objects at this same period, three men of earnest spirit and holy lives, named Zachary, Ferrar, and Morrigia, founded in Milan the Congregation of the Barnabites, and helped on the reforming work with great fruit among the poor of the towns and country villages.

All these men, be it remembered, whether Oratorians, or Oblates, or Theatines, or Barnabites, were one and the same as children of the Church—all preached the same doctrine, said the same Mass and the same prayers, made the same three vows of poverty, chastity, and obedience, and were subject to the same head, the Pope in the Roman See. They are therefore not in any way like the numberless sects of the separated Christians, who are each independent of the other, who have no common doctrine, no head or central authority, no intercommunion, no principle of cohesion, and have divided up Christianity among themselves into hundreds of fragments, until they have become the wonder and the jest of the heathen. Our Divine Lord might in truth say of them, as He said through His prophet of His executioners, "They have divided to themselves My garment, and over My vesture have they cast lots."

6. There were not wanting too in this century of reform others who set themselves to instil new vigour into the older religious Orders. The ancient eremitical Order of the Camalduli were induced by Paul Justinian to engage in a more active ministry, in keeping with the needs of the time. Peter Bassi rallied the Franciscans, and formed an extensivo branch of the stricter observance now so well known in many lands as the Cappucini or Capuchin Friars. They profess to carry out to the letter all the difficult counsels of perfections, so minutely described by our Lord, that have seemed to the worldly-minded so impossible of fulfilment. Anyhow, they showed to the sixteenth-century generation that there were yet men in plenty left in the

Church able and willing to tread this high and rugged pathway of self-immolating sanctity. They are doing it still.

7. But of all the men who left deep and lasting marks upon these and subsequent times, and did yeoman service in the Church, Ignatius of Loyola, the great founder of the Jesuits, merits the first rank.

When Pope Paul III., who set up the commission of inquiry into the discipline of the Church, was scanning a horizon dark with religious trouble, and feeling his way through the tortuous paths of political complications to assemble a General Council, there came to him out of Spain an ex-soldier, now in clerical garb, limping from a wound received in battle. He had a long and strange story to tell him, and some proposals to submit for his sanction. He was the youngest son of an old and noble family in the north-west of Spain. He had been a page in the royal retinue at court, and then embraced the military career. He held rank as an officer, and saw some sharp and dangerous service. He liked his calling. He was filled with the ambition of military renown. He had a zest, too, for the gayer pleasures so sought for by men of arms. When the French nvaded his country, in the war between Francis I. and the Emperor Charles V., he was with the

army of defence near the frontier. It fell to him
to command a forlorn hope in the fortress of Pam-
peluna, closely besieged by the enemy. When a
breach was made he sprang upon the crumbling
wall, and, sword in hand, was cheering on the
defenders, when some heavy masonry, hit by a
cannon-ball, came down upon him, shattering both
his legs. Struck with his bravery, the captors
gave him the honours of war. His wounds were
attended to with the rough surgery alone available
in such a place. He was placed upon a litter and
sent to his father's castle. He had to submit to
further cruel operations, and suffered agonising
tortures—hard for us to realise in these days of
anæsthetics. He bore it all without a murmur,
in the hope, as he tells us, that his soldierly
carriage and figure might be saved him, and
that he might not lose favour in the eyes of the
fair Castilian maiden whom he loved, so utterly
worldly was he then. The tedium of convalescence
brought a need for reading. He tried all kinds,
and, like all worldly minds, fell back only as a
faute de mieux, on the serious and the pious sort.
Then comes the long story of his conversion. It
is no ordinary one in his case, for his was an
ardent and passionate nature, brave withal and
resolute. This soul-story, which is also a fascinating soul-study, is told in great detail in any one

of the numerous biographies of him written in
every tongue. We come now to the days when he
had finished his studies for the priesthood in Paris.
His wonderful character had attracted to him some
able and promising companions, who made for him
a kind of following by tacit consent. He led them
one day to the crypt of a quaint little church on
the Hill of the Martyrs, and induced them to join
him in vowing the rest of life to the service of God.
As the service of God in this world is necessarily
the service of the Church, he then proposed, disciplined soldier as he was, to set out for Rome
to take orders from the commander - in - chief of
that service. He had, however, matured a plan
to be submitted. With a strategist's eye he had
scanned the world as his field for combat. First
of all, the motto on his ensign was to be the celebrated *Ad majorem Dei gloriam*. For him and his
there was nothing worth while striving for, nothing worth gaining but that. For that they were
—first, to combat ignorance and vice; second, to
prevent both, by educating the young—educating
them in all branches of science, even the highest
attainable by the human mind, but step by step
with the science of God and the soul, never fearing
that one could hurt or clash with the other; third,
they were to organise bands of men to go about
instructing the poor in the country and directing

souls among the higher class; fourth, they were to
send others into heathen lands to carry the light
and civilisation of Christ's Gospel to the idolaters
that sat in the darkness of the human life that is
without hope; and fifth, all was to be done under
the immediate command and at the bidding of the
Pope. Such was the man who came to Paul III.
in the year 1540. He had hung up his soldier's
sword long ago at a shrine of Our Lady. He came
now girt with the sword of the Spirit to ask for
his commission. There were those near the Pope
who were for not accepting. There were too
many Religious Orders already—there was scarcely
room for any more. Could not these men be in-
corporated in some other already established? and
so forth. But the Pontiff, though aged now, was
once a prince and a practical man of the world.
He looked upon that lame soldier; he knew him to
be a brave man. He liked a brave and resolute
man. Who does not? So he extended his hand
in blessing over him, and accepted him and all his
plans. Such was the humble beginning of the
great Order of the Jesuits. There was not a word
in all this about combating Protestants. Ignatius
never mentioned them, perhaps did not even think
of them. Often it happens that the most successful service for God is done by those who don't
know what they are wanted for. But certain it is

that Ignatius and his famous company have been a most powerful stay against the havoc wrought in the Church by the Protestant separation.

However, that the blessing of God was on his work is evidenced by the marvellous, well-nigh preternatural, and rapid growth of his Order.   Before the Saint's death there were over 6000 members of it in 400 houses, spread through many countries. One hundred years after there were 15,000 in 800 houses. In another century, 1773, there were 20,000 in 1000 houses, and to-day, though they have been persecuted like Him whose name they bear, driven out of nearly every country, and even suppressed for forty-one years by the authority of the Pope, they are again honourably restored, and number 18,000, scattered in every quarter of the earth, engaged in the same noble mission bequeathed them by their founder, and under the same motto, " A.M.D.G."

It has been said, and truly said, that in the rise of this illustrious Order, the Church has more than gained what she lost by the Protestant defection. In that you will find the key to the little love our separated friends have borne them. They were able to marshal such an array of talent and learning and eloquence against all comers, that their adversaries, like men driven to bay, have taken to the mean weapon of reviling and evil-speaking. It will for ever be a blot upon the fine literature of the English tongue, this envenomed abuse of the Jesuits. They are even turned into an offensive adjective in its dictionaries, whose meaning is unblushingly given as "cunning, crafty, lying"! And they never defend themselves. Personalities are not worthy of their metal. They fight not man. They only fight the vices of his fallen nature. I remember when "The Black Robe," by Wilkie Collins, appeared, a Jesuit Father of distinction came into our parts to advocate a local charity. I drew his attention to this unfair, unmanly, and foul slander on his Provincial in England. "Would he not notice it and vindicate himself in a court of law?" I asked. "Ah, my friend," the good old priest answered, "were we to answer every charge laid at our doors, we should not have time to do anything else, and you know we have other and better things to do." True, I did know.

"The casuistry of a Jesuit," or "Jesuitical casuistry," have become stereotyped as an English phrase. There is cant in that—there is more, there is great ignorance, and, besides, it is ungrateful cant. The sole end and aim of this so-called casuistry—the name given to the moral treatises of Jesuit theologians—is consolation and encouragement to the repentant sinner, the quiet-

ing of the fears that lead the timid of conscience
to melancholy and despair, and the veiling of the
awfulness of divine justice with the mercy of the
Redeemer. These, and these alone, are the motives
of this casuistry so sneered at. This mild moral
system has a history. The Jansenists of the last
century had fashioned a hard and galling yoke
for souls—a cold and rigid doctrine much akin to
the sour Calvinism of total depravity, making the
run of people think it well-nigh impossible to be
saved. There was Scylla and Charybdis in this
—despair or its reaction, total unbelief. To meet
this deadly peril the Jesuit masters of the spiritual
life advanced their more lenient and larger views,
and made them good in able works. In aid of
them too, they were the first to encourage devotion to the Sacred Heart of the Saviour, raising
up before a world discouraged by this withering
Jansenism this symbol of all that is gentle and
tender and forgiving, and bringing back a spring-
time sunshine of gladness to many a soul. They
have earned for this the gratitude and the applause
of the entire subsequent generation of Catholics.
Yet this is Jesuit casuistry and tricks. For shame!
Just take a practical common-sense view of this
wonderful organisation, and the prejudice possess-
ing some men against them will appear in all its
unreasonableness.

In the Society of Jesus there are subjects from many different nations. There are Spaniards, Italians, Germans, French, Belgians, Hollanders, Austrians, Hungarians, Armenians, Syrians, Russians, Poles, English, Irish, Scotch, Canadians, Americans, and Australians. If 18,000 men thus composed could conspire to deceive mankind, and could make themselves appear to be what in reality they are not, it would be the greatest moral miracle known. They must then really be what they profess to be, that is, religious men bound by those three self-sacrificing vows which sever them from every human tie and human ambition. They are intelligent men. They are not only well educated but highly-trained men. There are among them men eminent in every branch of human knowledge. Besides this, they subject themselves to a novitiate of rigorous discipline, where they learn to renounce and to obey. They know no home but their convent, no relations but their brethren. They must not elect any place or country for their dwelling. The wide earth is their portion. They may be sent to any part of it. They are in Red Indian countries, among the negro races and the yellow Orientals—two hundred years ago Father Ricci was as good as Prime Minister of China, and Father Verbeest erected the Imperial Observatory in Pekin, which

K

may still be seen—and everywhere they work by
rule and under the will of another. What do
they undergo all this for? If the Order gained
the wealth of nations, no individual Jesuit would
be a penny the richer for it. When a Jesuit dies,
all he leaves is a pair of old shoes and some rather
threadbare garments. That is his vow of poverty.
People who do not know them cannot believe they
do it all for nothing, so they smell dark designs
and plots, and speak in vague hints of enemies
to the human race. But there is nothing secret
about them. Their "Rules and Constitutions" had
the public approval of the Church, and are published. There is not the remotest Jesuit house
whose inmost recesses would not lie instantly
open to any one bearing one autograph line from
Leo XIII., authorising inspection. These men individually would be the veriest fools to devote
themselves to their hard life for merely dark
designs of ambition and intrigue, for they never
have anything but their food and lodging, and
just decent raiment. What they gain, or hope to
gain, by labouring to help their fellow-men in their
perilous journey to the borderland and beyond it,
is the great reward of the Master—the life eternal
for themselves. And can you fancy them jeopar-
dising that by doing the very things they are
ever dinning into the ears of others not to do,

for the very reason that they involve its inevitable forfeiture ?

But why were they suppressed by Pope Clement XIV., and remained so for forty-one years ? That is a long story, ably told and explained in the monumental work of M. Cretineau Joli, a French layman, for those who wish to follow it. I am not so foolish as' to present them as a band of angels or supernaturalised and impeccable men. Though they are expected to be and are above the ordinary run of us in goodness on account of their profession and vows, there is no state or station in humanity above frailty and mistakes. But whatever failing of imprudent zeal or unwise abuse of worldly influence there may have been on the part of members of the Order here and there which drew down censure on the entire body, this must be felt and said by all—that their unmurmuring submission to this fearful and humiliating sentence is their particular glory. They did not rebel or run away with the Catholic Bible under their arms and start a Christianity of their own, as the Protestants did—how welcome their accession would have been to the good haters of things " Romish " and " Popish "—but the Jesuits knew better than that. These 20,000 men, like a loyal *corps d'armée* under a cloud, resigned their colours and tendered their swords, and left their cause to God and time.

And the day came when all Christendom rejoiced
to see that cloud uplifted, and they that were
under it unfurling again their old standard, bearing
still the same device, *Ad majorem Dei gloriam*.
Ay, truly, "these be the valiant men of the house
of David" (2 Kings xxiii. 8).

I am not a Jesuit, nor have I been trained or
taught by Jesuits. But I have studied their history, and what I have said of them is the result
of that study.

On a certain Sunday, in this latter half of our
century, I saw a vast audience assembled in the
splendid Cathedral of Notre Dame in Paris. It
was composed exclusively of men. I should say
from their appearance they were all men of the
learned and professional classes. In fact, they were
the *savants* and *philosophes* and the unbelievers of
that centre of free-thinking. Their presence was
a tribute to superior talent, the genius of oratory.
Its representative was a son of St. Ignatius—the
celebrated Père Felix, the foremost orator of France.
That figure in the black robe stood alone above
that strange gathering. For a whole hour they
listened to the silver tones of a rare and polished
eloquence breathlessly, save when an involuntary
murmur of applause marked the ending of some
fine period. What was his theme? He was
appealing to these sceptics of the nineteenth century

for God's greater glory, as Ignatius ordered his first Jesuits to do 300 years before.

Another time I strolled into the Gesù—the mother Church of the Jesuits in Rome—on a Good Friday. The devotion of the Three Hours was going on. There could not have been less than 5000 people present, for after St. Peter's the Gesù is the most spacious, as it is one of the most beautiful churches in the world. On a raised platform beside the unveiled cross, stood the well-known black-robed figure again. The service was a beautiful one. The soft, slow chant of the season from invisible choirs filled the air with sad yet sweetest melody. In the intervals the single voice of the preacher was heard reciting the story of the Passion —the tears on many an upturned face told how eloquently. Up beyond that preacher, raised above the altar, there was a silver shrine chased in gold and gems. As I looked at that shrine and thought of him whose venerated remains lay preserved therein for now 300 years, it seemed as if the living voice I listened to came from that dread presence, and that Ignatius was still alive and working in the world for God and for souls.

PART V

THE CHURCH'S FINAL ANSWER TO
THE REFORMERS

WE now come to the time when the Church, in solemn council assembled, was able to gather all her strength together to combat, and, if possible, conciliate her rebellious members in this sixteenth century. Her action in this respect was necessarily limited. It could only consist in reaffirming and re-annunciating the body of doctrine preserved under the promise of divine guarantee in the tradition of fifteen centuries. This was the sacred trust committed to her keeping. Of this she was but the guardian, not the author. The author was Christ. He gave it to the apostles. They gave it to their successors, with the charge to teach but not to change. Therefore, in the doctrines preserved in that tradition, no concession, no compromise, no paring away, or removing was admissible. That was not her function. It was beyond her office. It would be interfering with divine authority, and that she could not—dared not do.

With matters of discipline, mere management of details of Church life and practice, and the abuses and detritus from the human element, it was different. With these things she was freer to deal. They were the outcome of the exigencies of the passing ages, and had origin in her own legislation or the defect of it. And with these she did deal firmly and edifyingly in the Council of Trent, besides publishing once more, clearly and unhesitatingly, a statement of the whole doctrine necessary to be believed to belong to her Unity. Nothing less would have come up to her duty of re-assuring and restoring confidence to minds much shaken and disturbed by these gusty winds of doctrine blowing about rather fiercely these five-and-twenty years. More she could not do.

As we learn from the 15th chapter of the Acts, even in the infancy of the Church, when any discussion or crisis arose, the usage was established by the apostles themselves of coming together and giving a decision about it. And in announcing the decision in the instance given, the remarkable words used by St. Peter, who presided, indicate the belief that such assemblies were and would always be under the guidance and guardianship of the Holy Spirit : "It hath seemed good to the Holy Ghost and to us," he said.

The practice of holding councils was continued in the Church as occasion, from the waywardness of human minds and human frailty, arose. They were the chief mainstays of unity, and safety-checks upon the questioning, disputatious, novelty-loving, and restless human intellect.

This was why the reigning Pontiffs, as well as the Catholic monarchs, notably the head of civil society in Europe, the Emperor Charles V., looked forward so anxiously to this great remedy for the religious troubles that broke out in so many quarters in the sixteenth century. It was only after nine years of negotiations that Pope Paul III. was at length able to invite the Patriarchs, Archbishops, Bishops, and leading divines of Christendom to assemble with safety in General Council. The place chosen was a kind of neutral ground. The little river Adigio, descending from the Tyrolese Alps, winds through a fertile valley just beyond the northern Italian border, in what is now Austrian territory. By the left bank of that valley river, surrounded by high limestone hills, stood an ancient town of some 10,000 inhabitants, called Trent. For over five hundred years it had been independently ruled by a Prince-Bishop, but was now federated, with home rule, in the German Empire. It was selected to please the Emperor, and as a sign, too, of fairness and goodwill to the

German people, from whom chiefly all these religious disturbances had come.

Towards this little town in the Tridentine valley began to journey from the remotest parts of Europe —from the distant East, too, and from the farthest Green Isle of the Atlantic—the Bishops of the ancient Catholic Church, in the year 1545. They rallied for the danger that threatened the old faith. They wanted to hear what were those strange innovations proposed by the daring and noisy men of Germany, and were determined that no profane or sacrilegious hand should be laid on the foundations of the ancient edifice, whose builder was Christ, and whose corner-stone was Peter, while they were by to protect and defend.

In those days of difficult travel they took long to come. So that when the first session was held in the venerable Cathedral, not more than thirty Bishops were present from the various countries, though gradually and finally as many as 281 took part, besides many hundreds more of representative men of lesser grade.

This was the eighteenth General Council of the Church. The Pope was not present in person, but he appointed three Cardinal Legates to preside in his name. All three were men eminent for their prudence and scholarship, and of tried virtue. Two of them were afterwards elected Popes, and the third,

Cardinal Pole, was of the royal blood of England, once the friend and intimate of Henry VIII., and now by him exiled and proscribed.

It is necessary to note the peculiar character of this assembly. It is in no sense a Parliament. A Parliament enacts new things and repeals old. A General Council imposes or invents nothing new in faith, and must not touch the old. Its office, as far as doctrine goes, is merely to declare what that Faith includes, or to explain and define more clearly any point of it called in question. It could not then, consistently with its mere character as guardian of what was divinely, definitely committed to its care, admit a party of debaters to discuss its truth, or justify their denial and rejection of it. It seems very evident that when Christ charged His apostles to go out and preach and teach, He must have made them fully aware of what they were to teach and preach,—otherwise it would have been a fool's errand indeed, considering the restless mutability of the human mind. Who so profane as to lower the wisdom and foresight of the Saviour below the level of the most thoughtless and improvident of men, especially when we think of the momentous consequences He announced as attaching to reception or rejection of that teaching —" He who believeth you shall be saved, and he who believeth not shall be damned " (Mark xvi. 9).

So the Protestants were not admitted to a share in
its deliberations. What would be the use ? The
members of that Council were convinced that what
they called in doubt and denied had been settled
once for all between Christ and His apostles
long, long ago. And if they were not so convinced it would have been injurious to our Blessed
Lord. And if the complainants objected that
in the lapse of time this teaching, by the accidents of human affairs, had been tampered with
and changed, that would be to give a flat contra-
diction to Christ, and impiously charge Him with
breaking a most solemn promise. He guarded
against such accidents. He promised to be with
His teachers " all days, even to the consummation
of the world," and that He would send His Holy
Spirit to abide with them, and to constantly call
to their minds all things whatsoever He had commanded them to teach. No, the complainants and
doubters and deniers were out of court ; they were
put out beforehand and for all time by Christ Himself. They had no business in a General Council.
Yet they were encouraged to come, not to argue
their case, but to listen to the grounds on which
their action was condemned, and at one stage of
the Council certain representative men of them
did put in an appearance. They looked for compromise and concessions. They were told that in

dogma this could not be. That all reasonable
complaints they had to make about scandals and
abuses—sad fruits of human frailty which had
crept into Church life—would receive a respectful
hearing; that they knew very well, just as well as
all Catholics, that there was nothing in the dog-
matic teaching to warrant incorrectness or scandals
in private conduct—all the other way. There was
nothing in all that teaching that did not tend to
righteousness, and there was everything that condemned and reprobated the contrary, and that the
Council felt it to be its duty to act in that spirit.
Its reformatory decrees of discipline still extant
are ample evidence of the truth of this. Now, if
these men were really and only anxious about good
and edifying living in the Church, surely they
should have been satisfied. But they carried
their protesting much farther and much too far,
until we feel inclined to say with the sceptical
man in Shakspeare:

"Methinks the gentlemen do protest too much."

The perfect order, thoroughness, patience of re-
search, and minuteness of details that marked the
proceedings of this Council commend it to our
respect and bespeak its earnest sincerity. No one
who glances over the authentic volume of more than
350 pages, containing its Canons and Decrees, the

latest edition of which was published at Rome in 1862, can fail to be impressed with these things. Do not go to that untrustworthy and one-sided and garbled account given as a so-called history by Paolo Sarpi, so favourably received and lauded by Protestants—suspect anything *laudatum ad hoste.* It is spiteful on the face of it. Read the volume of Canons and Decrees itself, and the order of procedure there laid down. These were drafted by the Secretaries of the Council, and bear the *imprimatur* of Pope Pius IV., under whom the Council was brought to a close. If you want the detailed and long story of the *transactions,* it is well to mention that the only book recognised by Catholics is Pallavicini's monumental work. Nor would it have been necessary, most probably, to write such a history at all were it not for the publication of Sarpi's untruthful statements. Sarpi's book had to be smuggled over to London for publication, and saw the light only a hundred years after the Council. Then the archives of Rome were opened to this learned Jesuit, Father Pallavicini, and he was ordered to give the world the real and authentic story in refutation of Sarpi.

Again, there is no better way to show clearly the sincere and truly religious spirit which animated this solemn assembly than to quote the wise words of counsel and exhortation which prefaced its deli-

berations. They were read at the second public
session, and are as follows :—

"This Sacred and Holy Council of Trent, lawfully assembled in the Holy Spirit, and presided
over by three Legates on behalf of the Apostolic
See, recognising with the blessed Apostle James
that every best gift and perfect is from above, coming down from the Father of Light, who gives
abundantly to all who ask His wise guidance, and
knowing at the same time that the beginning of
wisdom is the fear of the Lord—hereby declares
and enacts that all the Christian faithful assembled
here in Trent are to be exhorted to abstain from
evil and repent for past sins—walking in the fear
of God—not yielding to sensual desires—to be in-
stant in prayer, to confess their sins frequently and
partake of the Holy Sacrament of the Eucharist, to
visit the churches, and as much as possible to sanc-
tify the Lord's Day—also to offer private daily
prayer for concord among Christian princes and for
the Unity of the Holy Church.

"It is also enacted that the Bishops and Clergy
taking part in the General Council should assiduously offer prayer and praise to God, celebrating
the Divine Sacrifice of Mass at least every Sunday,

that day on which God made the light, on which
He rose from the dead, and on which He poured
upon Apostles the gifts of His Holy Spirit, thus
as the same Holy Spirit prescribed through His
Apostle, making supplications, prayers, interces-
sions, and thanksgivings for our Holy Father the
Pope, for the Emperor, for kings, for all that are
in high station, and for all mankind, that we may
lead quiet and holy lives, enjoy peace, and witness
an increase of faith.

"All are exhorted, moreover, to fast at least every
Friday, in memory of the Passion of our Lord, and
to give alms to the needy. In the Cathedral
Church on each Thursday shall be offered a solemn
Mass with the Litanies, to implore the gifts of the
Holy Spirit, and in all other churches similar
prayers. During the time of such services in the
city all idle visits and conversations are to be avoided,
and all are to assist at them, at least in heart and
mind.

"And as it becometh Bishops to be without re-
proach, prudent, chaste, and ruling well their own
house—it is enjoined that before all things there be
sobriety at table, and moderation in eating, and, to
hinder idle discourses, that parts of the Scripture
be read at meal time. They are to warn their servants and retainers to observe becoming behaviour,
to avoid occasions of sin, and in dress and bearing

to give that good example of righteousness expected
from the servants of the servants of God.

"In this manner the light of Catholic truth shall
shine amid the darkness of the heresies which these
many years have spread in many places, and through
the help of Jesus Christ, the true Light, whatever
needs reformation shall be reformed—and by the
skill and mature deliberations and diligent studies
of those assembled, whatever is to be condemned
shall be condemned, and whatever is in need of
proof, proof shall thereof be given, so that through
the whole world God and the Father of our Lord
Jesus Christ may be glorified with one voice in the
same confession of faith."

There is about that the right ring of sincerity
and earnestness, of unselfishness and impartiality,
strongly appealing to the respect of every man earnest or sincere himself.

Then there was no haste about this Council. It
protracted its calm and slow deliberations, with two
interruptions caused by political and insanitary
troubles, through eighteen years and the reigns of
three Popes. Surely such thoroughness and prudent
wisdom must carry great weight with serious minds.

From the decisions of this General Council,
published in great detail, we learn what were the
points of belief from which the dissatisfied and

protesting parties wished to free themselves, and what the assembled Church said in reply.

No little anger and indignation has been displayed over the frequent occurrence of the word *anathema* in the book of the Canons and Decrees—" it is full of curses, and cursing is, to say the least of it, not conciliating to one's foes." On the part of scholars this must have been said in very bad faith, and guiltily to mislead less well-informed people, for anathema is not a curse—it is a declaration. It is a Greek word, made up of a preposition and a verb, and simply means *placed outside* or *beyond*. Thus understood, the reading of the decrees is natural and matter-of-fact; if any one say " so and so," or deny anything contrary to this teaching of the Church, let him be anathema, that is, reckoned beyond her pale—outside her membership, which they who believe, of course, deem a great misfortune, but which those who *want* to be outside do not account a curse.

Well then, the various points of doctrine brought under the notice of the Council as advanced by the German innovators, were met, and properly met, with this mark of anathema on its authors. Their teaching was declared to be strange—it did not belong to the Church, neither did they. For instance, the dissatisfied asserted that the Bible was a book given to all, should be used freely by all to

L

shape their belief and learn their religious duty,
and that it was sufficient for that purpose without
extraneous aid or intervention.

The Council pointed out that though the Bible
contained divine revelation, it was a book that
needed the guardianship of skilled and divinely-
appointed interpreters.   It was more a revered
book of reference than an oracle speaking plainly
to each reader.   If it were the only and sufficient
guide, all men should have been born able to read,
just as they were born able to eat.   If it were true
that the Bible alone was sufficient, Christ would not
have established a visible Church, and commissioned
a body of men to go forth to teach.   He need not
have promised to be always with those teachers, or
have sent His Holy Spirit "to keep them in mind"
of what they were to teach, and to keep them from
making mistakes about that teaching.   All this,
however, He did do.   Besides, if the Scripture was
to be the sole guide, He should have composed that
part called the New Testament Himself, and delivered it to the world while He lived.   But our
Lord never wrote a line.   Not only that, but no
word of the New Testament was written at all for
twenty years while the *Gospel* was being preached
and taught, and some parts of it were not written
for sixty years after the Church had been founded.
How, then, could it possibly be the only rule of

faith ? Finally, the Bible not being an easy book to understand, to abandon it to the private interpretation and judgment of every one would prove most dangerous, if not fatal, to unity of belief.

How true this last forecast proved to be, let any one see for himself to-day in the hundreds of contending sects that are such a pain and puzzle and sorrow to all good souls—all the outcome of this private interpretation and judgment of the Bible alone. Even in such an early stage of the separation as Shakspeare's time, that keenest of observers perceived this disastrous result :—

> " There is no damnèd error
> But men will bless and prove it with a text."

Hence the Council could not admit their contentions about the Bible. It was the property of the Church. It was her text-book of instructions, and only that. It was she who preserved it through the ages with reverent care, who translated it, who had the most likely sources of information about its component parts and editions from her long unbroken traditions. It was a most vain and presumptuous pretence for junior innovators of that late sixteenth century to take it out of her hands, to set up any claim or exclusive right over it—in fact, it was stealing it and running away with it from its lawful old-time preserver and

owner. No, the Protestants might take copies of
the Bibles with them out of the Church, but that
gave them no right to it. How could they be sure
that they had even the right version at that late
day ? At any rate, it has proved an edged-tool in
their hands, and has cut up their Christianity into
two hundred jagged fragments.

In a long chapter the Council gave wise instruction about the Bible, and appended, after
lengthy, patient, and learned investigation, a full
list of the books of it to be henceforth deemed
canonical or authentic, no matter what outsiders
and unauthorised meddlers were to say on the subject. That list, and that only, all Catholics still
accept.

The discontented Germans put forth another
contention about justification. The Church's theory
about it hitherto was not easy enough or convenient
enough for lazy human nature that dearly loved its
self-indulgence. " Did not Christ once and for all
justify us by His sufferings and infinite merits ?
What, then, is all this trouble that is so uselessly
imposed upon us ? What is the use of all this
elaborate system of spirituality, and ritual, and
sacrament, and sacrifice, and penance, and prayers,
and fasts, and the rest of it ? Draw on His merits
by faith in Him—all the rest is but men's torturing
and tyrannous inventions." That would certainly

be all very nice and easy, and we can readily understand how seductive it is to the multitude.

But the Council calmly pointed out that Christ
our Lord did not authorise that view of it. Though
He paid the great price for our redemption, and put
all His merits at our disposal, He plainly placed
conditions for their application to us, to be fulfilled
by ourselves. If He had done all, and required us
to do nothing, why did He say, " Unless a man be
born again of water and the Holy Spirit he cannot
enter into the Kingdom of God "? (John iii.). Why
did He say, " Unless you eat the flesh of the Son of
man, and drink of His blood, you cannot have life
in you "? (John vi.). Why did He command us to
pray, and give us the example of it? Why did He
give the Apostles the power of forgiving or retain-
ing sins — of loosing and binding (Matthew xvi.
and xviii., John xx.), if He once for all removed
the sin and the bond? Why did He multiply moral
stories or parables about repentance and good
works, and bid us "go and do likewise"? Why
did He say that " a cup of cold water " given in His
name should not lack its reward, if we could never
merit anything?

Again, the dissatisfied Germans objected to any
one form of faith being essential to salvation, or any
one Church having a monopoly of salvation. The
Council reminded them that Christ was not of their

way of thinking—"he who believes *what I commission you to teach* (and nothing else) shall be
saved; he who does not believe it shall be condemned." Could He have put the issue more briefly
or more strongly than that, or have made the meaning plainer?

They could not tolerate, either, the idea of men
claiming infallibility in anything.

The Council was just as much opposed to infallibility in human affairs as they were. But in the
case of a divine revelation replete with mystery,
and in face of human minds restless and fickle, the
Council pointed out very clearly that nothing less
than immunity from mistakes in handing it down
would suffice. That is all that infallibility amounts
to. Only a very unreasonable person could object to
that, and only a very unreasoning one would attri-
bute such a want of wisdom to God as not to provide
thus against mistakes or deception. What more
natural to expect than that when Christ commissioned men to teach for Him, He would see to
it that, amid the accidents of human things, they
should teach exactly what He wished and only
that?

They were especially impatient, too, those lovers
of their independence, of the Pope's monopoly of
authority, of his primacy and supremacy.

The Council quietly showed that in this capacity

he was only representative, and that submission to him and allegiance were given not to him as a man, but to Christ, whom he represented. That representing the person of Christ was a historical fact in St. Peter's case. To him He first made over His full authority. The succession to this high office passed to St. Peter's inheritors in the Roman See. This was also historical and but natural. What can subsist in this world without a central and fixed authority? In the State, in all civil life, in the army and the navy, order, discipline, and safety rest on one solid recognised principle of authority. And is the Church and the spiritual kingdom of God and souls to be alone in this world without what is felt as a necessity all round—abandoned to the wayward caprices and whims of every comer and goer, faddist and theorist, spouter and crazy man that may elect to raise his voice? It is not common-sense. The primacy and supremacy of the Holy See are as essential to the preservation of Christ's kingdom as an axle is to wheels.

It was thus, point by point, patiently and laboriously reasoning, honestly and slowly investigating and setting forth the grounds of all the Church's claims and the credentials of her mission, that the great Council of Trent answered the dissatisfied and separating German reformers, and

through them all others who choose to act in like
manner. The investigation was exhaustive, and
the answers complete and final. They have been
before the world now for 300 years, and there
is not a Catholic of the 240,000,000 to-day who
does not hold and subscribe to them still. The
closing of this Council and the promulgation of
its Decrees by Pope Pius IV. mark the parting
of the ways between the Catholic Roman Church
and her dissentient children of the sixteenth century. Except in individual cases—and they were
many everywhere — those ways for the nations
have drawn no nearer together. For the first
time, in this waning nineteenth century of ours,
there has come to men a sense of uneasiness, if
not of shame about it, which may lead ultimately
if slowly to better things.

CONCLUSION

Now let us take a practical view of the religious situation as it stands to-day, and reckon up all the things that should be done to bring about a united Christendom. The mind grows faint at sight of the discordant elements that lie around. So opposed, and often so bitter, is the feeling that divides the various bodies still calling themselves by the Christian name, so wide and long continued their separation, and so manifold the interests engaging the thoughts of each, that the task of bringing them again together in one confession, under one head authority, seems, and well may seem, to human eyes but the wildest of dreams. Yet, if we lift our eyes for a moment from this distracting spectacle, and rest them only on principles, the thing seems not only feasible but easy.

No one can dissent from the axiom that you can have no unity nor united action of any kind in this world without one fixed and firm centre of authority. If you take the experience of a single human person, or a single family, or a com-

munity of persons, or a society, or a state, or a
country, what good are they all without a head?
The human person, without the material head, is
but a load of useless, inert members. Countries
and governments without the analogous moral
head soon go to useless pieces, and never come
to anything. By a stronger reason the same is
true of religion. As a nation without a governing
head is said to be in anarchy—a thing that
people so justly dread—so religion without a recognised governing head becomes an anarchy too,
and of the most fatal kind.

But why not let it be with religions as with
nations—each independent of the other with its
own head? It works well in the one case, why
not in the other? Yes, that would be a likely
and easy solution, only that the Divine Founder
of the Christian religion said nothing about a
plan of that kind. He appointed one chief for
all while He lived : " Peter, lovest thou Me more
than these?—Master, Thou knowest all things, and
Thou knowest that I love Thee—Then feed My
lambs and feed My sheep." If that .is not ap-
pointing a chief pastor, what is? If it were
in the divine plan of things that Christ was
never to go away, that He was always to remain
visibly displaying His God-like power, there never
would have been any question of this headship, nor

of a good many other things. But it was not in
that plan. So He appointed one to take His place,
and only one. "Thou art Peter, and upon this
rock I shall build My Church." He knew full well
that Peter in turn should die too, and that His
Church was to last. So He plainly meant that
there should be succession in that headship representing Him through all time. Therefore, it is as
certain as that there is a Church, that this head-
authority and representative is, and must be, among
us now, and that is the head and the centre round
which all must rally for Unity if they want it.
There is no other way of getting it. Now you see
we have narrowed the intricate question a good
deal. Narrow it a little more. Who is head, if he
is here in the world at the present moment ?
Where is he to be found ? Find the answer, and
you will be very near the solution. It cannot be
very hard to find out—if so, why is it not done
and admitted ? Well, it is here history comes in.
It tells us that for a long time, nearly 1000 years
after Christ, there was no manner of question or
doubt of who he was and where. The Bishops
who in regular turn succeeded St. Peter in the
Roman See were universally regarded as the living,
visible head of the Church. This is no *ex parte*
statement. It is written plain and large on the
page of history for anybody with eyes to read—

while each Roman Pontiff was a living fact, easily
authenticated by contemporary generations. It tells
us then, that after this time certain members of
the Christian family in the East got into a dispute
with this central authority, withdrew their allegiance, and threw it over. Thence the separation
of the Greek-Russian Church. Later on, others
nearer to this central authority in the West
did the same, and proceeded to set up independent Churches of their own in a few countries,
which are since known as the *protesting* or Protestant nations. Thus the great rent was made
in Christian Unity. Now, when it comes to the
question, as it has come in our days to many serious
minds, of restoring that Unity, and the first thing
to consider is, where shall be found the governing
head around which to rally, who in the world has a
better right to that office than he whose predecessors were in unquestioned possession of it before
the Christian world for 1000 years, and who at
this moment is yet acknowledged in that character
by a perfectly-united Church of over two hundred
million members? It seems, does it not, an easy
step for the descendants of those who are separated
from him, and whose position thereby becomes, by
the law of evidence, at least suspicious, to acknowledge him once more and be re-constituted in the
one fold? Yes, it looks easy, and in principle the

right thing to do. But looked at practically there is nothing in the world, humanly speaking, more difficult to bring about. That this should happen it would be necessary for the richest and proudest hierarchy in the world to transfer allegiance in spirituals from the Czar of all the Russias to the present occupant of St. Peter's See. The patriarchs of Moscow, Constantinople, Armenia, Bulgaria, and Roumania should seek renomination from Leo XIII., and bid their numerous suffragans and clergy, and their flock of ninety million souls, to look Rome-ward for all jurisdiction again. Are we likely to see that stupendous change? When we look far-ther west in Europe, things are still more compli-cated. In the East, Sacraments, the Mass, and all ritual substantially are the same as in Catholic times. But in Germany, at least in two-thirds of it, in Scandinavia, in Denmark, in England and its world-wide Colonial offshoots, there is scarce a vestige of the old Catholic creed that has not been whittled away to meet the exigencies of private judgment. Besides accepting all the ritual and discipline and practices of the Catholic life, which the Greeks never wholly abandoned, they would have to recast and build up anew their whole confession of faith.

Yet the present Pope has invited them all to return to the ancient Church. He makes no

detailed proposals, and suggests no means of bringing it about but one, and that one contains the virtual
admission that such a wished-for consummation is
not within the scope of unaided human power. He
asks all to pray that God may deign to do it.   No
one yet holding by the supernatural should refuse
that prayer, for this religious dissension among
Christians is a terrible and momentous question.

"Master," said the man in our Lord's parable,
"did you not sow all good seed in your field?
Whence come, then, all these bad weeds?" And he
said, "An enemy hath done this!" Who is the
enemy? It imports all men to know, for whoever
he is, he has inflicted a great wrong on the Divine
Sower, who watered that seed with His own blood.

When our Blessed Lord stood in solitary prayer
in the shadow of the olive trees of Gethsemane,
a vision of all future time was unfolded to His
human soul by His divine power. Far in that
future, without any doubt, He saw the present hour
of our world to-day. He heard, too, the noise of
multitudinous disputings with all their acrimonious
recriminations, slanders, and misrepresentations from
lips that invoke His sacred name—He saw the
hands of men stretched out in angry contentions
over the seamless garment of His truth, until they
rent it into a hundred fragments, flaunting its
shreds and rags in each other's faces, to the scandal

of the world and the sorrow of His angels. It was then surely at sight of this direst among the woes of time, the big, round beads of blood stood out upon His sacred brow. It was then, in the silent solitude of that night-hour, that He cried in His anguish, " O Father, see how My soul is sorrowful unto death. Oh, take this cup of agony from My fevered lips ; do not ask Me to drink—nevertheless, not My will, but Thine be done." And that cup of mysterious divine permission to men to work all their wicked will on the spotless Church He founded—He had to drink to the dregs, and then, convulsed in the sobs of His great sorrow, He fell forward along that garden pathway, waiting for the visiting angels to comfort Him. Like unto those angels of solace, and as dear unto Him, will be the earnest workers who shall contribute in ever so humble a way to bring about in our day the Reunion of the Churches.

Now, it is asked every day from many quarters, how far is the Catholic Church prepared to go— how far *can* she go in concessions to those separated from her if Reunion is to take place ? Well, she can concede, if she chooses, everything in purely disciplinary matters enacted in laws made by her, or introduced by custom and sanctioned by her. Thus, celibacy of the clergy might be repealed. She could modify or abrogate ecclesiastical fasts

and abstinence, also her marriage laws regarding
impediments.   She could modify or change devo-
tional practices, and the rules and constitutions of
Religious Orders, so as to make them easier.   She
could make large concessions in ritual and cere-
monies, and so forth.   But when it is asked if the
Pope is to renounce infallibility in teaching faith
and morals officially, *i.e. ex cathedrâ*, or if he shall
cease to assert his primacy of honour and jurisdiction
over all the Church, or if the Mass is to be declared
superfluous, and the Eucharist only a memorial containing no Real Presence, or if Purgatory and the
Indulgences are to be never more mentioned, the
Catholic Church will assuredly say " No." And
it is just as well the separated should know it
from the outset, and not look in any vain expecta-
tion for compromise on these and like *doctrinal*
matters.

THE JEWS

This conclusion I feel would be incomplete without
a word about another and no small religious factor
in the world of our day, and, for the matter of that,
of all days known to history.   The Jews must be
counted when we speak of Reunion, because it is
a prophecy of Holy Writ that before the end they
are to be " gathered in."   St. Jerome, in his Homily

on the second chapter of St. Matthew, says that "the Jews, at the end of the world, receiving the faith, will be enlightened." This declaration is founded on St. Paul's words in his Epistle to the Romans (xi. 26, 27), who in turn founds his statement on what is prophesied by Isaias in the fifty-ninth chapter of his book in the Old Testament. They are to come back, then, to the Christ they first rejected as a people.

It is to be remembered that the nucleus of the Church was entirely and exclusively converted Jews. All the apostles were converted Jews—and the eight thousand converts after St. Peter's first two sermons were all Jews. Jews, then, are our progenitors in the Christian faith, and in fair proportion throughout the Christian times they have been dropping in as our brethren; and as the number notably increases we may reasonably take it as a sign that the world is rapidly decreasing its distance from its *dies iræ*. When the end is at hand no more Jews will be left. In a French Review of recent date a certain Dr. L. Leaze has a striking article to show, first, that the Jews of our time are fast leaving their religion for Christianity; and secondly, that when they do come in, they are gradually taking command of it, so eminent are the places they and their descendants are winning for themselves in the Christian communions. And he cites numerous

M

instances in support of both contentions as having occurred in recent years in Prussia and Austria, in Russia and Poland, and most notably in France. All this supports our theory of the gradual fulfilment of the prophecy, and also, if true, brings nearer to our horizon the dreadful dawn of the great ending.

THE END

BURNS AND OATES, LIMITED, PRINTERS, LONDON.